From 1945-1952, Japan was occupied by America. It was America's most significant experience of being a colonial government. For the Japanese, it was a period of suspicion and humiliation. For the Americans, it was a chance to experience a people they had only known across the battlefield. Despite the brevity of the contact, some Americans left with a lifelong love for the country.

This is their story.

KAMI + KAZE
神と風

A スタジオウェナ Production
Austin, Texas, USA
www.wenapoon.com

ISBN-13: 978-1495921032
ISBN-10: 1495921034

神と風

スタジオウェブ

BOOKS BY THE SAME AUTHOR

Lions in Winter (2007)
The Proper Care of Foxes (2009)
The Biophilia Omnibus (2009)
Alex y Robert (2010)
Novillera (2013)*
Maxine, Aoki, Beto & Me (2013)*
Kami + Kaze (2014)*

*featuring original photography

(forthcoming)
The Adventures of Snow Fox & Sword Girl
Voyage to the Dark Kirin
The Marquis of Disobedience

KAMI + KAZE
神と風

絵物語

with black and white photography

WENA POON

スタジオウェナ

In memory of my great-grandparents
whose marriage was interrupted by this war

杨专炎　高清微
天长地久

KAMI + KAZE
神と風

A story of Occupied Japan

"You'll get a Japanese driver."

She looked up from her files, surprised. "I can drive," said Kate.

Her boss was unperturbed. "All Allied administrators our level get free servants. They're paid for by the Japanese government."

"'Servants'?" she said, making a face. She signed a document at her desk.

"I get four. You get two. A maid and a driver. If you don't need a driver, you can have two maids. Do you want me to tell them to make the change? Your house will be ready on Friday."

Kate was tired. It had been a rough initiation the moment she arrived in Japan. The radiator at the hotel didn't work. The water from the taps ran brown. She had been up all night, thirsty, shivering under uselessly-thin cotton blankets. "This embassy dinner tomorrow," she closed her eyes. "Do I really have to?"

"It's your call. My wife really wants to meet you. She's so bored here." Charlie strayed by the door. "Actually, all the wives are really curious about you."

"Why? Because of my dad?"

"Hell no, they haven't heard of him. It's because we haven't had any Californians. What's more, after you graduated from Radcliffe, you *actually went to work*."

Kate stared at her boss for a moment, then started laughing.

Charlie's eyes twinkled. They had known each other in college. He was two years her senior, in the men's college on the same university campus. They were in a theater group that put up Gilbert & Sullivan operas. She played the Captain's daughter, Josephine, in *HMS Pinafore*; Charlie, the poor sailor Ralph, who loved her more than life itself. Good times.

Charlie said, "The Ambassador's wife wants to you to join her Thursday afternoon book club. She also privately asked me if you were lesbian."

"Lesbian?" Kate exclaimed. "What on earth – ?"

"Any woman who isn't married and who consents to an overseas posting is either a lesbian or a whore."

"I believe the traditional distinction is *madonna* or whore?"

"Opt for lesbian," he urged. "Lesbian makes all of the wives feel safe."

"Doesn't make sense. Won't I prey on them?"

"As long as you don't prey on their husbands. Anyway, the wives move in a pack," Charlie made a shape with his hands of a travelling herd. "You can't pick them off as easily as you can the men."

She screwed up her eyes and said, "Well, I haven't decided yet on my sexual orientation. I'll file a report with her when I know."

"At least decide on your domestic help! What's it going to be? Two maids? I need to make a phone call. The Japanese get really flustered if you change the orders last minute."

"I don't need any maids, Charlie." She thought of her mother back in a lonely suburb. "But I know someone who does."

"Who?"

"Mom's living alone now in Menlo Park. If I get a maid, even a Japanese one, to look after her, she'll be able to come."

"To Japan?" said Charlie, surprised.

"It'll take some convincing. She hates Orientals. Gave me a hard time for accepting this job."

"It's not safe here."

"It's not safe *there*. I can't have her living alone. Our neighbors who look in on her every day are already in their seventies." Kate realized he was concerned about his liability for American families in Kyoto. "She won't be any trouble. She's not mobile anymore. Once here, she won't leave the house."

Charlie ran a quick calculation as an experienced administrator. If her mother was here, Kate might actually serve till the end of her two-year tenure in the public health department. "If you can get her to come to Kyoto, we can get someone to look after her, no problem. The hospitals are improving. We get really top notch guys. She'll have American medical care."

Kate shook her head. "She's not sick yet. I just need someone to watch her at home. She tends to fall down. Vertigo."

"I'll have to put in an elegant, official reason for why your mother needs to be shipped to Occupied Japan. Maybe, 'Consultant to the postwar effort – Harry Schroeder's ex-wife'?"

"Works for me. Can she come by plane? The ship'll kill her."

"I'll see what I can do. And – no driver, two maids?"

"Yes sir."

"You want a side of french fries with that?"

"Go home, Charlie."

Charlie grinned and turned to leave, then paused at the door. "I'm so glad you are here."

Kate emptied out the dusty drawers of her desk and filled it with new stationery. "I hope I last. I'm not worried about the job – it'd be the same anywhere – it's more the living conditions."

"The food situation is getting better. You should have seen when I first came."

"Yeah. Thank God I'm not allergic to soy. I read that it's in everything." She frowned suddenly. "Tofu – what is it?"

"Oh, it's good," said Charlie enthusiastically. He searched for words. "It's like a – paste."

Kate grimaced. "A paste? Made of soy?"

"No, no, it's – um, more like a flan."

"It's sweet?"

Charlie gave up. "Just try it," he said sagely.

❀

She went to meet her mother at the military airport.

Word had gotten out that a very important, elderly American lady was flying in and may be in need of medical assistance.

"Mom!" she waved.

Glenda stepped carefully down from the airplane onto the tarmac. She was wearing a beautiful pink suit and matching pillbox hat. The wind snatched at her little veil.

"Hello kiddo! Like my flying suit? Got it just for this occasion. I feel just like a movie star," she said. Her voice was hoarse from a lifetime of smoking. "The wheelchair kinda ruins the photo opportunity."

She went up to the Japanese staff. There were twelve men and women, all from Kate's office. They had been waiting patiently. One even brought an oxygen tank and mask. Glenda put her large Mark Cross bag in the wheelchair. "He can carry my handbag in that! Ha!"

Kate smiled. "Be nice, Mom. They just thought you might be tired after the long journey."

"They're so…little! Look, I tower over their men! I'm like Gulliver in Lilliput!"

Kate said in warning, "Mom – "

"Do they speak English?" she inspected the staff cautiously.

"Yes," said the Japanese, and bowed together.

Glenda's hand flew to her mouth. She was genuinely mortified. "Ooops. Sorry. Didn't mean to be rude. You know what 'Gulliver' is? It's a children's book – "

Kate's Japanese secretary welcomed Glenda to Japan and wished her a pleasant stay. Glenda asked her where she leaned English.

"Bryn Mawr College," replied the young woman, blushing.

"Oh!" said Glenda. "We have a very good school by the same name in America!"

Kate burst out laughing. "C'mon, Mom. Let's go before you embarrass me further."

The staff bowed again deeply as they left. Kate explained bowing to her mother.

The Japanese driver took them slowly through the traffic, down pleasant, tree-lined avenues.

"I thought we bombed Japan to kingdom come," said Glenda, looking out the window.

"Not Kyoto."

"Is the air dangerous? Is there radiation? Is my skin going to peel off?"

"No. But there's a lot of TB, diphtheria going on, and the water's unclean. As long as you take basic precautions, you'll be fine."

Glenda made a face. "Mrs Vitale was sure I was going to die here. But I said, 'if it won't kill the kiddo, it won't kill me.' She said the Japanese here aren't like the ones in Palo Alto. They're more Oriental because they haven't been, y'know, modernized," she darted a look at the driver and lowered her voice. "The Orientals are very excitable by nature. She read about it in a literary magazine. If they don't like anything, they dash their brains against a wall in protest. It's true, isn't it? They're really suicide-prone. Like the *cammy-katzy* pilots. Seen any of those here?"

Kate shook her head. "Everyone here's focused on staying alive, I assure you."

"Oh, I loaned Mrs Anderson your piano. We got the gardeners to help us move it. Since we're both gonna be here for two years."

"That's fine."

"Pianos need to be played, you know. Otherwise they go all sour." Glenda pointed out the window as they rounded a corner. "What's that? Is that where their little Emperor lives?"

"No, that's just a temple."

"And that?"

"Another temple."

"And that?"

"They're all temples, Mom."

"What kind of god do they worship?"

"It's not just one." Kate explained Shinto and Buddhism.

Glenda said heathens gave her a headache. "I'd

be missing Thanksgiving and Christmas. I don't suppose Orientals celebrate?"

"No, but we do."

"Are there enough Americans to party with us?"

"More than you'd ever want to meet," said Kate. She rattled off the military's statistics of personnel stationed in Japan. Glenda pulled out a pack of Lucky Strikes from her handbag. Kate snatched it away, rolled down the window, and flung it into the road.

The driver nearly stopped the car.

"Katherine Ann Schroeder!" cried Glenda, annoyed.

"You promised."

"I'm in Japan, for God's sake. Surely the ban doesn't extend to Japan?"

"It's a worldwide prohibition."

"What a waste," grumbled Glenda. "It was unopened."

"Someone would have picked them up already. We're short of cigarettes here. Don't worry, they won't be wasted."

The car pulled up to the front of her wooden, two-storey townhouse. It had previously belonged to an old professor who had escaped to the countryside during the war. He had passed away. Although traditional-looking, the house had been built with a few modern conveniences, including a Western-style bathroom. Such houses were coveted by the US army looking to buy property for their personnel.

A Japanese woman of about fifty was at the front door. Despite the cold, she looked as if she had been standing outside the whole time, waiting for their arrival. She was clad in a plain, dove-grey kimono with a purple belt, her hair perfectly coiffed. She bowed deeply. This time, Glenda mirrored her and bowed back.

"*Ohaiyo gozaimasu*," said the Japanese woman. "*Margaretto desu*."

"That's all hello?" said Glenda. "That's gonna be hard for me to remember."

Kate turned to pay the driver. He was a young man she had not seen before. He looked embarrassed when she handed him the money.

"Is it too much?" she said. "How much is it?"

He bowed and spoke up for the first time. His English was impeccable. "You don't have to pay me. I'm very sorry I did not have a chance to explain. My name is Nakamura Shinji. You can call me Timothy. This is my mother, Miko. You can call her Margaret. We were assigned to your house. Charles Robertson-san, he filed a requisition order for two maids, but meanwhile, we had already packed everything and moved here based on his previous order. We came ahead of schedule. The house needed a lot of cleaning. But don't worry, we have organized everything for you. The maids will arrive by seven o'clock tomorrow, and my mother and I will be transferred. I am sorry for any inconvenience."

"Maids? What maids?" said Glenda suspiciously. "You lined up a huge welcome party, kiddo."

Kate studied Shinji and Miko for a while. "Oh, man. I'm sorry to cause this logistical nightmare. I was trying to go for less, not more."

Shinji bowed. "No problem at all, Schroeder-san."

"Please call me Kate. My mom's Glenda."

Miko helped Glenda into the house. The women mimed to each other the removal of shoes and made an elaborate pantomime of bowing to each other.

"It is really not a problem," said Shinji. "Although I think, it is better for Kate-san to have a driver, than drive the car herself to work."

"Why?" she said sharply.

Shinji lowered his eyelashes. "Because it is better."

"Because I'm a woman?"

He looked like he was carefully choosing the right words in English. "Please don't misunderstand. It is more efficient."

"Why is it more efficient to involve two people, when one person can do the job?" asked Kate. She was known for this philosophy at the office. It was why she was promoted quickly.

"Have you noticed? Kyoto has a traffic situation. There is always some problem on the road," said Shinji. "If I drive, Kate-san can do her work in the back before arriving in the office. It is a better use of Kate-san's time."

She studied him coolly. It was true. She had a ton of reading to do, reports to edit. She had arrived on the heels of a huge public relations disaster of the Allied forces in Japan; she had to fix it quick.

"My mother had nurse training during the war,"

said Shinji.

"Is that right?"

He pulled out a letter from the inside pocket of his black suit jacket. He wore gloves. He presented the letter to her with both hands. "This is her testimonial from the hospital. She cannot speak English, but neither can the two maids that are coming tomorrow." He unfolded another piece of paper. "This is a letter proving my prior employment at ATIS, GHQ, SCAP."

"ATIS?" asked Kate.

"*Hai.* Allied Translator and Interpreter Section, General Headquarters, Supreme Commander for Allied Powers." He bowed. "I also drive."

Kate took his letters, scanned them briefly, and smiled at Shinji. "You've thought of everything."

He opened his dark, caramel-colored eyes very wide in a mute appeal.

"I'm gonna drive Charlie crazy, changing the thing again," said Kate, kicking off her shoes and going into the house.

"Don't worry, Kate-san," said Shinji. "I will call Robertson-san's office."

"Yes, do that. I'll make it your problem, since you have the most incentive to get that sorted. And thanks."

Kate went into the kitchen, where Miko and Glenda were already miming to each other recipes.

❀

The car that was requisitioned for her was a Japanese model. It looked ten years out of date. Hardly any passenger cars were produced during the last years of the war, so the car did not surprise her. The portable radio inside, however, was unusual. Her young driver informed her that it was his property. It was hand-built from random American parts and housed in a polished wooden case, with a nifty plastic strap. He had acquired it on the black market. He was very fond of listening to it during the drive. He tuned in to the Far East Network, broadcast in English by the US armed forces from Tokyo. The jubilant propaganda that came over the airwaves did not match the Kyoto she saw from the car window. Still, she let him leave it on. Listening to it was part of her job.

The morning program was called *Enjoy Your Time In Japan*.

"Please remember to behave with propriety at all times," the strong, cheerful baritone of the American male announcer came over the airwaves. "Whether you are members of the US armed forces, or representatives of the US government, you are always in the public eye. Be careful of how you dress, and how you appear. Do not offend our Japanese hosts. It is important, for example, to be sensitive to superstitions, isn't that right, Kayoko?"

His Japanese female co-host said gaily, "That's right. For example…"

An extended discussion of popular Japanese superstitions.

A tiny sigh of exasperation from the driver's seat – "Huhhh."

Kate looked up from her papers. "You don't agree with the radio, Shinji?"

"Stupid," was all he said.

"Really." She leaned forward with interest. "Who's stupid, the man? The woman?"

He shook his head, as if explanation was beyond him.

"You don't agree with their discussion of Japanese customs?"

He agonized silently for a while, then blurted, "It is not even that. It is the way they speak. Her English is so bad. And his Japanese – he cannot even say *arigatou gozaimasu*. So simple! He says is wrong, every single time! Who allowed these two people to be on radio every day? They hurt my brain. They waste my battery."

Kate smiled. "Turn it off then."

He reached for the knob. "They should just play music."

❀

Kate worked long hours at the office.

"Is it worse than you thought?" Charlie knocked on her doorway.

"Sixty-eight infants dead," she said, lifting a sheet off the desk. "Over five hundred seriously ill. We look like shit, Charlie."

"It wasn't our fault. It was a Japanese company

that made the vaccines."

"Yeah, but American doctors stuck the needles in. They always believed our injections would kill them, and now their worst fears are confirmed. Anyway, why are you still here?" she retorted. "Don't you have a wife and kids?"

"She's out at the book club. The kids are asleep by now. Coffee? It's good. From my secret stash. I just made a new pot."

"Why not. Can't sleep anyway."

He called from the pantry. "Insomnia?"

"It's really noisy outside at night. Last night, there was a fire in our neighborhood. It was small, but everyone poured into the streets to watch the firefighting. I mean, what's there to see?"

"They're paranoid about fires."

She sighed. "I think it's just being in Japan."

He came in with two mugs. "You'll get used to it."

They went over the proposals outlining the amount of reparations the government would have to make to the victims' families. Kate had to draft another speech.

"How are your Japanese servants?" asked Charlie.

"They're fine," she said briskly, inserting a new sheet of paper in the typewriter. "Mom says Miko is 'nice, for an Oriental'. Shinji looks like a girl."

Clack, clackety clack-clack.

"I thought their names were Margaret and Timothy?"

Kate made an impatient noise as she consulted her notes and typed quickly. "You know they did that for us. Forget it. Anyway, why say three syllables when you can say two?" She glanced back at him when he made no answer. "What?"

"Just the speed at which you type. It's astonishing. I remember being so impressed when we were in college."

"Yeah. Remember that old fart, Professor Walberg? He used to compliment my penmanship and my typing. He said I had all the hallmarks of a great secretary."

Charlie chuckled, sipping coffee. "Who cares about him? He's long dead."

"Good. Hope he *stays* dead."

"Would you like to come to dinner with me?"

"When?"

"Tonight."

She glanced at the clock. "It's nearly eleven."

"There's a little shop in the marketplace that serves ramen. All night."

"Ra - ?" She lifted an eyebrow.

"Noodles."

"I can't eat wheat."

"They have other things."

She stared at him. "Charlie."

"Kate."

They had a silent conversation with their eyes. Then Kate looked back at the typewriter. *Clackety clackety clack-clack, ting!* "I was afraid when I got your letter that I was not being selected by your office because of my resumé."

"'Course you were," said Charlie quickly.

"I gave up a really good career in Sacramento to come here, Charlie. Don't mess things up for me."

Clack-clack-clack, ting! She tugged at the carriage return. *Zzzhup. Clack-clackety-clack.*

He went over to stand beside her. Then he sat on the carpet beside her chair and rested his head against her legs. She did not move and continued typing. Slowly, he wrapped his arm around her right leg, as if it were a pillar, and huddled close.

"Someone might come in," she said, looking down. She did not pull away.

"There's no one here." He sounded like a small boy. He flew planes in the war. All his brothers died except him. She was relieved when after the war she received news that he was alive, and that he was engaged to be married. She couldn't go to the wedding in D.C., but all their classmates went.

"How old are your girls?" asked Kate. She put her hand gently in his hair.

"Three and thirteen months."

"Do they look like you?"

"The baby does."

She smiled, staring out the window. There was a large moon that night. "How are they liking Japan?"

"More than their mother."

"What did Audrey use to do before she got married?"

"Nothing. She majored in American History. She collects antique teacups." He buried his face in the woolen fabric of her skirt. "She lives for the girls. I don't exist. I didn't know having children would do that to women."

"I wouldn't know," said Kate. She rose gently and sat on the floor beside him.

"I'm completely shut out. They have their little planet, it doesn't include me," said Charlie. "She liked me enough when we got married. Thought I was a war pilot. Then – it just faded. What did I do? I'm still the same, aren't I? Some of the guys, they get really fat."

"Still as handsome as the day I saw you on stage," said Kate, brushing the lock off his forehead. "It's not you."

She held him in her arms.

❀

Shinji darted looks at her in the rearview mirror.

"Am I driving too fast for you to write?" he asked.

"No," said Kate, marking up a speech. So many things one couldn't say. She stood before an abyss. Nothing could bring those kids back. It was a huge blow to the Allied effort. The American doctors were inconsolable; some asked to be transferred back. She was up all night working on this speech for a radio broadcast. Her task was beyond the realm of words. Even if she managed to strike the perfect pitch in English, how on earth would it sound in Japanese translation? Can sincerity ever cross such a huge gulf? The wind from the dark chasm roared in her ears, tore at her clothes. She sighed and put the speech away; pulled out another dossier.

"Does Kate-san want a blanket? There is one under the seat."

"Oh?" she reached for the fluffy woolen throw gratefully. It was starting to rain outside.

"What is Kate-san reading now? It is very thick."

"It's classified."

Kate looked out the window, then said, "I'm just joking, Shinji, don't look so hurt."

"Kate-san cannot see me looking hurt." He glanced at the rearview mirror.

"I can feel you looking hurt. I have special sensory feelers."

He did not reply.

"I'm reading a very long report about our efforts to import wheat into your country. We have a lot of wheat. We need to make you guys eat it."

"Japanese eat rice."

"Really?" she pretended to be astonished.

He said nothing.

She sighed. "There's not enough rice right now. We need to convince the Japanese to eat wheat, which is cheaper and just as nutritious."

"Wheat is not good for you. Kate-san herself does not eat wheat."

"That's because I'm allergic, it's not the same."

They stopped at a light. Shinji brooded. "Actually, what does 'allergic' mean?"

"It means if I accidentally eat something with

wheat in it – like noodles, or cake – I can get a severe reaction. I could die."

"From wheat?" Shinji was alarmed. "Japanese people could die from eating wheat?"

"No, no, no!" Kate was impatient. "Don't you go around saying that, please! Not after what just happened!"

"Kate-san just said wheat will kill her," he said stubbornly.

"It's not wheat that would kill me, it's my own body. It is something inside me, Shinji. Obviously not everyone is allergic to wheat, otherwise everyone in America would be dead by now. Why, you eat wheat."

"I will never eat American wheat," he proclaimed firmly.

"I saw you eat a chocolate muffin at the Embassy the other day. That's made with American wheat flour."

Shinji drove mutely.

"You didn't die," added Kate in triumph.

Finally, he said, "Chocolate muffin is nice. Bread isn't nice. The American advertising says we should eat bread for breakfast instead of rice and miso." Shinji turned round quickly and made a face at her. "Bread tastes like paper."

"Not good bread. If we buy an oven, Mom'll teach you how to bake really good bread. It's easy. Homemade bread smells like the best thing in the world. Just make sure I'm not at home when you guys take out the wheat flour."

They were now stuck in traffic. There was an accident. They were only half a mile from the office. Walking would have been faster, but from the ominous rasp of the windshield wipers against glass she could tell the rain was quickly turning to sleet. Finishing up her reports in the car, and conversations with Shinji, were now part of her morning routine.

"I still do not understand this 'allergic' thing," argued Shinji. "How can Kate-san be 'allergic' to wheat when Americans are not? Isn't Kate-san American?"

"That's how allergies work. People react differently to the same thing. It's impossible to predict sometimes. Don't you have any allergies?"

"No," said Shinji proudly. "I do not have such silly illnesses."

"Oh? I thought you had some medical condition, that's why you weren't conscripted during the war?"

He fell silent.

She could feel his embarrassment. She tried to stick to the earlier subject. "I know a girl who is fatally allergic to both soybean and rice. She wouldn't be able to come live here."

"Soybean! And rice!"

"Yes. Eating any of those things by accident would kill her."

"Not true!"

"It's true, Shinji. Why would I lie about such things."

"How can something we eat every day kill Americans?"

"Exactly. So how can something Americans eat every day – like wheat – kill the Japanese? What I'm trying to explain is that allergies are caused by a…a condition inside our bodies that cause us to reject a substance. *People* are the problem. The thing itself is not poisonous. Understand?"

He shook his head at the rearview mirror, an apostle of another faith.

❀

Charlie kissed her furiously. The clothes were coming off.

"Don't. It's a wooden house, there are three other people here," said Kate firmly, catching his hands.

"Where can we go?" he whispered desperately.

She thought for a moment. They were in her bedroom. Downstairs, she could hear Miko talking to Shinji, preparing dinner. Shinji translated for Glenda. Laughter. The Japanese wooden house had virtually no sound-proofing. It sounded as if the people downstairs were in the same room with them. And there were neighbors on both sides of the wooden walls.

"The car," she said. "It's parked in the next alley. Come."

They clattered down the narrow stairs.

"Mom, Charlie's going out for a cigarette," she called, pulling on her winter coat. Charlie did not stop for his and was already outside, waiting. "We'll be right back."

"Wish I could join you!" rasped Glenda.

It was not very comfortable in the car. In the tight, dark space, they made love quickly, urgently, afraid of being discovered. Fortunately the alley was deserted. The low skies threatened to unload more snow. They hoped few people would be out at that hour.

"I don't want to move," said Charlie. They were under the blanket.

"I could sleep here, right now, for a thousand years," she said.

"Why can't we just say fuck it, start the car, drive away. We'll go to another town, change our names."

"The other towns are all fucked, Charlie. People are still dying from simple things."

Sober thoughts of the situation in Japan, heard daily on the news. A huge flood had buried several coastal villages in a nearby prefecture; medics were rushed to stop the spread of disease. In Kyoto, the Japanese staff in the office had been going to the funerals of the dead babies all week. Kate hugged Charlie closer, desolate all of a sudden. Why had she come to this country?

Charlie shifted his weight and kissed her. "Kate?"

"Hm."

"I don't think she would even care if I asked for a divorce. Her parents have money."

"Don't. Your kids are so small."

"I don't think they'd notice."

"They notice," said Kate. "My dad left us for another woman when I was two. I knew. Mom said I kept asking for him for years afterwards. I did get to see him regularly when I grew up. But it wasn't the same."

They were silent for a long time. It was so warm under the blanket.

"Sometimes I wish I'd just died in the war like Jeff and Tom," said Charlie. "I know it sounds completely stupid and corny. Everyone keeps saying how lucky I am. Even now. They think I've made it. But what's the point." They stared out the window. A few snowflakes were hesitantly making their way down to earth. "What's the point. I supposedly fought for freedom but ended up more trapped than I had ever been in my life. And look at the mess we made here. Look at the clean-up job."

"There's no choice *but* to clean-up."

"Why didn't you get married after college?"

"Haven't met the right person."

"If you got married, I don't think you would have made a name for yourself the way you did."

"Probably not. I would have poured my energy into my family. My kids." Kate frowned. "It's not wrong, what your wife is doing. Loving your kids, that's the same as loving you, isn't it?"

"I can't talk to her about anything important," he said regretfully. "I wish we dated in college."

"You never asked."

"What do you mean?" smiled Charlie. "I confessed my love for you every evening, and twice on Sundays. You never noticed."

Kate laughed. "None of those lines ever seemed real."

"Damn the Savoy operas!"

"We better go."

"Wait," he said, holding on to her.

"They'll be wondering."

"Just the space of ten breaths. It's so perfect, Kate."

He watched the snow tumbling down, breathing slowly, savoring each breath.

One. Two. Three.

Four. Five. Six.

She looked at the man beside her and realized then that this was the first and the last time they would ever make love.

Eight.

Nine.

Ten.

❀

"Brrrr!" she laughed, sliding open the front door. The house smelled of boiling leek, simmering fish.

"Where were you guys?" demanded Glenda. "I'm starving. Miko wouldn't let me eat first."

They gathered around the hearth. There was an iron pot suspended from the ceiling. A cast iron fish served as a hook.

"So, for dinner we have…" announced Glenda importantly, looking over the dishes. "First, the soup. Do not be fooled by its humble coloring, this soup is the *pièce de résistance* of dinner tonight. Miko scored some winter vegetables at the market. I do not remember any of their names, they are all some kind of carrot or onion, and because they are Kyoto carrot and Kyoto onion, Miko says they are super expensive, so please eat your vegetables boys and girls. Please note the gummy cubes in the soup: in case you mistake it for an American minestrone, kind sir," she nodded at Charlie. "The gummy cubes will remind you that you ain't in Kansas anymore." She indicated a plate. "Here we have the appetizer, which I helped prepare, and which I call Fishy Circles. This is entrée number one: Fishy Squares. Entrée number two: Fishy Tubes. They're all fishy things, just in different shapes, right, Miko?"

Miko tittered with mirth.

"Am I not right?" demanded Glenda of her cook with false belligerence. "Begone with your fishy squares and fishy circles. I want Spam!"

Shinji translated for his mother, although no translation was really needed for *Spam-mu*. "My mother says fish is healthy."

"Is she saying I'm fat?" said Glenda.

Laughter. Miko brought out a small, wooden tub of rice. A clink of rice bowls. Rice was a luxury; they all got neat portions carefully rationed by Miko's tiny bamboo spatula. The smell of steamed rice made the winter night seem colder outside; and the hearth much cozier inside. Charlie even brought a bottle of Cabernet from his stash. He unfolded the corkscrew in his Swiss Army knife. Miko brought out teacups. Nobody had seen a wine glass for a long time in this part of town.

"Miko, where are you going?" said Kate. "You and Shinji eat with us."

The housekeeper looked at Charlie and turned red. She seemed more shy around white men.

Shinji said awkwardly, "My mom wants us to eat in the kitchen. Because we have guests."

Charlie told Miko if she wouldn't eat with him, he was going to leave right that minute. He even got up to go.

More laughter.

❦

The next morning, Shinji didn't come in for breakfast. He was already waiting for her in the car. It had been washed and polished. It gleamed black against the snow like a brand new patent leather shoe.

"Are the roads closed?" she said, as he opened the door for her.

He shook his head silently. After she arranged herself and her papers in the back seat, he held out a white handkerchief. In its crisp fold, one of her earrings.

"Oh," she said. She was wondering where it was.

He bowed curtly, folded his handkerchief neatly into his pocket, pulled on his gloves, then got behind the wheel.

Shinji sulked during the entire drive.

❀

"Earthquake!"

"Everyone under the table!"

The overhead lamps swung wildly. Pencils rolled, files toppled, splashing papers all over the floor.

"*Ouuuaaah!*" cried the Japanese women.

"Don't worry," said Kate. "It's okay, it's okay."

The shaking intensified. Framed maps leapt off the walls and crashed onto the floor.

"*Daijoubu,*" said the Japanese men to the women. "*Daijoubu.*"

Kate was under the table with her Japanese secretary. As the tremors continued, her secretary held Kate's hand to her heart, as if Kate was a child needing reassurance.

"It's okay," said Kate, trying to smile. "I'm from San Francisco."

The tremors ceased.

The staff of the office waited, wide-eyed and expectant, for any aftershocks.

"All right, everyone back to work," said Kate, patting her secretary and crawling out. "I think that was the last of it. We got off easy, didn't we?"

Everyone began tidying the place.

"We are safe because we are in a stronger building," said the Japanese secretary. "But wooden houses, they might have fallen down."

Kate looked out the window. In the distance, she could see trees where she couldn't see them before. Some houses had clearly collapsed.

Charlie appeared at the door. "Kate, go check on your mom. Everyone, go home for the day. Be careful!"

The staff grabbed their bags and winter coats and scattered.

"You all right?" asked Kate.

"Yeah," he hesitated. "I'd take you home, but I gotta check on Audrey and the kids."

She nodded. Pulling on her red coat, she grabbed her satchel and headed out into the wintry afternoon. The streets were filled with people hurrying about, school children crying. A siren began to wail.

"Kate-san! Wait!"

She paused as Shinji caught up with her.

"I was parked outside your office," he panted.

"Oh? I didn't notice."

"I always wait outside." He bent over, trying to catch his breath.

"All day? Until I get out of work?" she was amazed.

"Yes. More efficient. Driving back and forth wastes petrol."

She looked at the filled streets. "Useless to drive now, and probably dangerous. Let's walk home."

"Where are you going?"

"Isn't it this way?"

Shinji grabbed her hand and pushed through the

crowd. "Kate-san never noticed the direction of her own house. Because I drive and Kate-san never looks up from her papers."

"You're right. I haven't a clue."

"Quickest way is to cut through the temples."

It was an astute move. Few of the panicking passersby thought of going into temples during such a situation, and the courtyard of each shrine yawned empty. The courtyards were all linked. As long as the gate at each end was not bolted, they could cut across town effortlessly.

They heard shouts in the street. "We better hurry," said Kate.

"Don't worry. The house is strong," said Shinji grimly.

"I'm worried about Mom."

"My mother will take care of her."

She felt bad all of a sudden. He had a mother, too, and like her, his mother was his only relative, as far as she could tell. A curious symmetry of lives.

They reached a brick wall and a tall set of gates that were firmly locked. The attendant had disappeared to help with the crisis outside.

Kate hiked up her skirt and began climbing.

"Kate-san!" Shinji cried, astonished. "Let me go first!"

"Come on, it's not that difficult." She wore sturdy ankle boots with small heels. She kicked snow off the ledges and made her way carefully over the top. She leaned over and saw Shinji fretting at the bottom of the gates. "Come on, Shinji, don't be a sissy!"

He scowled. Seizing the iron bars with his gloved hands, he leapt and swung himself easily over the gate. The courtyard on the other side was lined with silent maples, their delicate, tangly branches encrusted with snow from the night before. It was difficult to believe they were still in the heart of a bustling city. They crunched hurriedly through the untouched snow.

"Is 'sissy' the same as 'girly'?" asked Shinji.

Kate apologized. "I was joking. You know I love you, Shinji."

He turned red.

"That's also a term of endearment," she said hastily.

"You have no right to make fun of me. Kate-san is not much older than me."

"Why, how old are you?"

"Twenty-eight."

She was shocked. She had assumed he was much younger. It was always that way with the Japanese.

"I am not a child," he said pointedly. "I went to good schools. I would have graduated with a diploma if it were not for the war. Why do you think I can speak English? Americans are always so condescending."

"Oh, come off it, Shinji, you know I'm not like those guys!" said Kate. "I'm sorry, okay?"

"You are really sorry?"

"Yes."

"Then come." He pulled her hand and hurried

her up the steps of the temple.

"Where are we going?"

"To temple."

"But – "

"It will take one minute."

"What for?" she almost screamed with impatience.

"Come."

She ran up the flight of steps of the brooding, black temple. It wore a fringe of snow on its undulating gables, like the eyebrows of a white-haired sage. Beneath her boots, each broad step was made up of a single tree trunk cut square and laid horizontally across. If it were still a living tree, she would not be able to get her arms around it.

"Where did they get so many gigantic logs?" she marveled, falling behind Shinji and measuring the width with her boots. "Oh my God. Look at how wide this trunk is!" They were not on a human scale. She felt like a midget.

"This temple was built very long ago. No such trees now. They would take another one thousand years to grow again this big. Please, take off your shoes."

Kate had never been inside a Shinto temple before. She always meant to go in, but didn't have anyone to take her. From the outside, they looked very formal and intimidating to a foreigner.

Shinji went up to an altar filled with various prayer tablets and offerings. *Clink!* He dropped a coin in a donation box and extracted a glittering thing.

"Stand still," he commanded. He held what looked like a jester's staff. It was a red cardboard tube rigged with tiny, golden jingly bells. He shook it in various directions around her head.

Jing!

Jing!

Jing!

"What are you doing, Shinji?" she said, her voice a whisper now.

"I am cleaning you of your sins."

"What!"

Jing!

"I am not sure if this way will work," he said seriously. "But, better than nothing."

She realized what was troubling him. The earring. It had been in the car. "What I do on my own time is my own business," said Kate quietly.

"The car belongs to the government of Japan. It does not belong to you. You should not use it for such things."

"Stop being such a prude."

"I do not know what 'prude' means."

"It means you are objecting to a woman sleeping with a man on moral grounds."

"Precisely," said Shinji. "Robertson-san has a wife and children. Is America so modern now that even that kind of behavior does not cause you any shame?"

"And Japanese men don't cheat on their wives?"

"They do. But right now, such adulterers are not telling a country what medicines they must take, how they should raise their children, and what they should have for breakfast."

'Adulterers'. What an ugly, precise word for what she felt for Charlie. But Shinji was right. A spade is a spade.

He gave her the wand. "Do this every day. To summon the gods. They will keep away bad spirits that prey on the sinful."

Kate took the wand warily. She was about to say something when Shinji turned away and bowed his head towards the altar. He shut his eyes in prayer. "Now, pray for the babies who died because of the vaccines."

She clasped her hands and shut her eyes.

They could hear fire engines.

❀

After the earthquake, Charlie and his family left Kyoto. Kate was promoted to Charlie's position as head of the department. It was an unprecedented move. In the United States, she would not have been allowed to lead or advise a group of men. But this was Occupied Japan, and she was the best talent they had.

She went to say goodbye to Charlie's family at the docks. It was the first time Kate ever saw Charlie's wife and kids. She wanted to come see them all off, even though he was against the idea. She felt it was necessary. She needed to have the right memories.

"You must be Kate!" said his short, pretty wife, shaking her hand. She introduced her children. Charlie was right. The baby had his coppery hair and blue eyes.

"You must be relieved to be going back to D.C.," said Kate.

"Oh, aren't we all! I'd been begging Charlie to get a transfer back to the States for ages! It's really not a place for kids, not with all the diseases going around. The earthquake was the last straw! I'm so glad you came out here! If you hadn't, I doubt they'd ever let Charlie go."

"Yeah," said Kate, her hands in the pocket of her overcoat. She felt ashamed. Audrey was not the cold, upper-class wife she had imagined. In real life, she shed a genuinely warm, benevolent glow. The romance Kate felt for her old classmate shriveled up into an ugly, forlorn thing. There was a problem that Charlie and Audrey had to fix. She was not part of the solution at all. "This kind of posting is best for singles."

"Charlie says you moved your mom here? Is she going to be okay?" Audrey leaned in and whispered. "It's so *dirty* here. I can't take it anymore. And so difficult to find good domestic help."

"Mom's fine," said Kate, smiling. "She's a real trooper."

"Is your father in the army?"

"He passed away. He was an army photographer."

Charlie came. "All right, guys! We gotta get on

this ship."

"Da!" cried the baby from the pram. He picked her up.

"Goodbye, Kate," said Charlie cheerfully. They had already rehearsed the night before. He leaned in and kissed her on both cheeks. "It's all yours now. Sally forth and conquer!"

Kate buried her face in the baby's cheek and smelled its cool, damp smell. She kissed the girl fervently. "Damn, Charlie, she's a carbon copy of you. Take care of her."

"I will," he whispered. "Goodbye, my fair Josephine."

"S'long, Ralph."

Then they were gone.

❀

Jing!
Jing!

Shinji sat on the wooden ledge at the front door of Kate's house. Shoes and clogs were lined up on either side of him. It was a clear night; a full moon rose above the jagged rooftops.

Jing!

Jing! came the slight tinkle from upstairs.

He smiled to himself and lit a cigarette in the dark.

❀

Kyoto, the following spring.

With the cherry blossoms came a large contingent of US army doctors, all very young, only in their mid-twenties.

Kate frowned over the latest progress report. "How," she said aloud in the car. "How, how, *how* do I get people to accept their vaccinations? Diphtheria is going through the roof. These children are dying so needlessly."

"Why should we trust any longer the American doctors who killed our babies?"

"It was a mistake, Shinji. And it wasn't done by these doctors, these are new guys, they're really good and they want to help." She sighed. "Fuck."

"Kate-san speaks terrible language. The Japanese ladies at the office are copying you."

"How do you know?" She scribbled something furiously on her memo pad, pursuing a thought.

"They boasted to me. Everything you do, they copy. You have to be careful."

They often had conversations like this on the morning drive to the office. It was a legitimate component of her work day. In exchange for promises to her driver that she would uphold public morals, he gave her, albeit grudgingly, insights on the local populace.

"I'm serious, Shinji. If I can't turn things around, we'll lose our funding. We'll be shut down, then *nobody* would be cured. I'll be fired and everyone will lose their jobs, you included." Kate punched the seat in frustration. "After all the trouble we took to get grants to pay for the vaccines! Now they're just sitting there in their sealed boxes. A vaccine is no use at all unless it's *in* a human being! It makes me sick, I tell you." She remembered the temple Shinji had made her pray in. "Hey Shinji, who can I pray to? Recommend me a Shinto god who can solve my problems."

He shrugged.

"Please! I'm willing to give it a shot. That temple you took me to, the day of the earthquake, is it the best temple in Kyoto? Take me there."

"I am not a tour guide," said Shinji haughtily.

"I'm serious. Which is the best temple in town for making your wishes come true?"

The reply came instantly: "Kiyomizudera."

"What-what? Where is that?"

"Outside Kyoto. On the mountain. Famous."

"It really works?"

"*Hai*," he nodded curtly. "The Shrine of Clear Waters. Provided you meet certain criteria, success is guaranteed."

"Guaranteed?"

"*Hai*," he nodded again. He looked very serious.

"What criteria?"

"You must have a clearly-defined wish, coming from a heart of true sincerity. And your soul: it must be *clean*."

"You don't think I'm clean?" she said wryly, chewing at the end of her pencil. "I've been cleansing myself with the bells you gave me. I'm spotless."

"And you must have faith. One hundred percent

faith." Then he said brightly, "I have an idea. Kate-san should hold a big ceremony for the people of Kyoto. All the newspapers should come. Make the new doctors line up at Kiyomizudera, apologize to the gods for their sins, and demonstrate their sincerity to heal the Japanese people by jumping off the balcony." Shinji chuckled at his own joke. "Then maybe the Japanese people would take them seriously."

"Because they jumped off a balcony? I don't get it."

He explained that the famous, broad terrace of the temple, the *butai*, was cantilevered over a precipice. The view of Kyoto from the *butai* was breathtaking. For hundreds of years, pilgrims dared themselves to leap off the balcony while making a wish. If they survived the fall, their wish would come true. It was literally 'a leap of faith'.

"God, sounds like stuff they'd do at the frat," marveled Kate.

"Frat?" frowned Shinji. "What is 'frat'?"

"In the boys' college – at my school – the men would do such crazy shit. While drunk."

"Being drunk will increase rate of success."

"You want me to get the army doctors drunk and leap off this balcony? You think it'd work? As a public relations stunt?"

Shinji nodded. She could tell he was trying his best to keep a straight face.

"Since when did you acquire a sense of humor, Shinji?" she leaned forward and prodded his shoulder. "Huh? Who are *you* copying?"

"Glenda-san!" He laughed so hard that he fell against the steering wheel. "I'm sorry. I was just imagining – all the American doctors – jumping off the *butai*. Ha ha ha!"

Kate fell back in her seat and pulled out her notebook briskly. "Where exactly is this temple again?"

❀

"What happened?"

Glenda was in bed. "Nothing," she said boredly. "I just fell down again."

"Look at that cut," said Kate, examining the sticking plaster on her forehead. "Was Miko at home when you fell?"

"No, I'd sent her out to the shops. Now she is in her room, blaming herself. Go check on her, please. I don't want her to, you know do that *curry kitty* thing." Glenda made a motion of stabbing her own abdomen with a blade. "She thinks she's responsible for me. Tell her I'm responsible for me. If God says it's my time, I go."

"Have you been smoking, Mom?" sniffed Kate.

"I stole Shinji's cigarettes."

"You *didn't*," said Kate in disbelief.

"He managed to get hold of Lucky Strikes," Glenda cackled. "Figured I'm just inching my way towards the finish line. Why not make it a last, mad dash."

"You're killing me, Mom. I'm going to cut you

some slack today because you're injured." Kate picked up Glenda's empty carafe and headed for the door.

"Hey – hey, kiddo, come back here." She patted her bed. "In case I just – you know – croak, I want to share something with you."

Kate looked at her suspiciously. "You're not my real mother."

Glenda laughed till she coughed. Kate had to thump her on her back. "No, no. Geez. No, I want you to find out for me – don't you have secret access, spy files, that kind of thing? I want you to find out for me who used to live here. Like, look up their names. Try to get photographs if you can."

"Why do you care?"

"I have this theory." She beckoned to Kate and whispered. "I've been observing them all these months."

"Who?"

Glenda pointed at the door, indicating Miko and Shinji. "Sssh. I have nothing to do all day when you're at work, see. So I just sit in the kitchen and observe. The way that woman cleans the kitchen, tidies the house – there is no way she hasn't lived here before. She makes a big show of hiding it, but I know. I mean, she knows exactly where the dust accumulates; she wipes the place with a ritual – just trust me, I'm a housewife myself. I know these things."

Kate was startled. "You mean she may have been the prior housekeeper?"

Glenda shook her head impatiently and motioned her to be quiet. "I asked her who used to live here, and she said a professor. Apparently he was a music professor."

"So?"

"I think she's the wife, and Shinji's the son."

"No way!"

"That's my theory anyway. That's why they wanted to work here so badly."

"That's terrible! They should have said something."

Glenda shook her head again. "Don't let on. The house doesn't belong to them now. They must have been desperately broke during the war in order to sell it in the first place. If you let on, you'll just embarrass them. You know how awkward it can get."

Kate nodded slowly, her mind racing.

"You know," said Kate. "I always wondered what Shinji is sick from, that he didn't get conscripted into the Japanese Army. Does he look sick to you?"

"No," said Glenda. "He didn't serve?"

"That's what he told us. He was the right age, so we asked. He has no military history."

"That's weird."

"I know."

"Was he exempt?"

"Apparently, because of a medical condition. What, I don't know, and of course he would never say."

Glenda considered. "Hm. I should stop stealing his cigarettes. What if he had been a psychopathic killer who ate GIs for breakfast in Okinawa? He could have come back and erased his file. Maybe you shouldn't ask him about his past, kiddo. He might become violent. With Charlie gone, who's going to protect us two little American ladies?"

"You're the one who started it! You asked me to go digging around for information."

"I'm just dying to know if my theory is correct. I might croak tomorrow, then I'll never know. I'll be haunting you to find out."

Kate was exasperated. "You should get a real hobby."

"Can we get an oven?" asked her mother hopefully.

❦

"Hurry up, Kate-san!" he beckoned from the car. "It's ending, quick!"

She had never seen Shinji so excited. He shut the door on her and leapt into the driver's seat. He turned up the volume on his radio. A colorful riot of orchestra and piano, ending in a declamatory smash.

"What is this music?" he turned around, his eyes shining. "They announced at the beginning, but I missed it. Do you know what it is? I heard it before. It's *fantastic*."

Kate said it was from some war movie.

"Hollywood movie?"

"I think it was made in England. The piano concerto is by Richard Addinsell."

"Addinsell?" He frowned. "I have never heard of him. He is a genius."

"He's a British composer. Originally they asked Rachmaninov, but he turned them down."

"Twice I have caught it on radio, nobody can tell me what it is called."

"The piece is called *Warsaw Concerto*."

"Warsaw?"

"As in Poland. They were invaded by the Nazis."

The radio was now broadcasting the news. Kate looked out the window. An old man sat, forlorn, in a street corner, his clothes in tatters. He stared at her silently as they drove past.

"What is the movie called?"

"*Dangerous Moonlight*."

He liked the name. "Did Kate-san see it?"

She shook her head. "It was really stupid."

"Why stupid?"

"It came out during the war. People needed fantasies. Not only is the Polish hero a World War II flying ace, he's a piano virtuoso."

"That would be okay in a Japanese film," said Shinji. "So, what happened?"

Kate scowled. "The usual. I think he falls in love with the heroine, fights the Germans in his plane, crashes. At some point he loses his memory."

"And?" asked Shinji anxiously.

"Oh don't worry, he wakes up in the end and remembers her. Happily ever after."

"I would have liked to see it."

"I heard the acting was awful. But the score's

good."

"Kate-san plays the piano."

"That's right."

"Can Kate-san play this?"

"I've never tried. I probably can do the easier parts."

"Yes, the beginning of the piano solo is easy. The B major theme. It is the best part. It is much better than the C minor theme, which is too much."

"Too much?"

"Yes, it is the B theme that is simple, restrained. It is the part that is genius." Shinji's voice glowed with approval. "Addinsell-san is very clever. Even though he pretends to show a lot, in reality, he does not show too much."

Kate smiled to herself and continued looking out the window. She said lightly, "Did you study music, Shinji?"

He fell silent. Then, "The hero, does he play this concerto in the movie?"

"I s'pose so. That was the whole point."

"I've never heard the beginning of this concerto. Only the end." He hummed it.

"Oh," said Kate. "It starts like this." She hummed it softly.

Shinji listened attentively. Then he hummed the orchestral part, and she did the piano solo. They drove through Kyoto, imagining a film they had never seen. Another war, fought in a different universe: thoughtful, voluptuous, heroic.

❁

She had to go to at least one book club party during her tenure. There was simply no avoiding the wives. The more she tried to dodge the bullet, the worse it looked. There was no longer any boss to shelter behind: now she was the boss. She looked at the list of titles they were doing each month; gritted her teeth at the options. The month of May was Agatha Christie. That might be worth her time. She had to rsvp long in advance so that a copy of the book could be procured for her from New York and flown to Kyoto in the next courier pouch.

"I'm taking a half day off," said Kate to her secretary at the office, gathering her things. "You hold the fort when I'm gone."

"Ah! The book club."

"This is just a one-time thing."

"*Hai*, Kate-san. Please enjoy."

"Got any bullet-proof vests?"

"Haha!"

The afternoon started out badly. Charlie was right, the wives may dislike each other, but when they attacked, they moved as a herd. All disguised attacks, of course – a little kick here, a bite there. She had expected this: what surprised her was the uniformity of viewpoints. She had hoped for some variation, the slightest indication of a kindred spirit, but nobody peeled away from the herd to sniff her out alone.

One of the older women alluded that young

Kate had taken a job opportunity away from her husband, who had been in Japan longer, had more experience of the 'natives', and was long overdue for a promotion. Another woman cracked jokes about the Women's Army Corps.

"Oh, the WAC is a riot," said the Ambassador's wife. "During the war, we practically ran out of birth control to hand out, because those girls were so 'hot to trot!'"

Shrill laughter. The sudden influx of professional women radiographers, stenographers, electricians, mapmakers, drivers, even co-pilots in the US forces during the war had not been a welcome development. It made the wives look bad. Worse, it freed up the men from safe, back office jobs. Those men got sent to the front. That was exactly what the government wanted, but not the wives. Military women, in short, were bad news for everyone. Cruel assumptions were made about their class backgrounds, upbringing, morality and ability to 'start families'. Kate picked her way through the landmines cautiously, hugging her rifle to her chest, a lone soldier in hostile territory.

"Are you married, Kate?"

They already knew the answer, but it simply served as a lead-in for the rest of the questions.

"But don't you want to have a family?"

Kate had a vision of the dinner at home she was missing at the moment: Glenda, Miko, Shinji, laughing over Glenda's latest 'localization' effort (origami); Shinji translating between the two women, or deliberately withholding or manipulating translations for comic effect.

"Oh, but I have a family," said Kate warmly. "My mom's here."

"It must be really stressful to be head of your department," said one of the wives. "With all the dreadful things in the news these days."

"Goodness, I wouldn't want to be in your shoes," said another.

Kate lowered her head and said, with appropriate humility, that it was a tough position to be in.

"They say you actually write the speeches for the men?"

She nodded.

"The guys say what you tell them to say? Is that allowed?"

"That's what I used to do in California," replied Kate. "I do the research, and I write the propaganda. It's just a job. Doesn't matter if a man or a woman does it."

The wives exchanged meaningful glances with each other.

"But how do the men stand it?"

"I know my husband would never say what I write for him!"

Again, that forced laughter around the group. Their eyes were tense, watchful.

Kate said, "Actually, it makes sense for my position to be filled by women. A lot of time-consuming things like reading and research, drafting and editing, are involved. It's a job for bookworms. You know our men. They're so impatient. They don't like spending long hours at the typewriter."

"True, true!"

Kate was a public relations expert. In a few deft strokes, she painted a portrait of herself as someone who performed ministerial tasks and served merely in a supporting role to the men. The wives had been mistaken: they had no reason to feel threatened by such a woman. She was charming and deferential. She sat with her knees together and a smile on her face the whole evening.

Cocktails arrived. The women reminded each other that it was, after all, a book party. They dutifully took out their copies.

"The part I thought was really interesting was – "

"I didn't like it when she – "

"I knew he did it, of course. It was obvious he was the murderer."

"You'd think she'd leave us in suspense for much longer!"

"Do you know in real life, Agatha Christie is a real adventurer?"

"What does her husband do?"

"Cigarettes?"

Kate blinked. The women were passing around a large carton. The embassy was never short of good cigarettes. She pulled out two packets and put them in her handbag. The Ambassador's wife raised an eyebrow but said nothing.

❋

Where were you all night? This crane's for you. Of course it's not as nice as Miko's. Shinji refused to make any. He said there is no point in making a crane or two: if one had to fold an origami crane, one had to fold a thousand of them and string them at temple shrines for luck. Shinji does not do things by halves. Tomorrow I'm going to try making a frog.

I've given up hoping for an oven, kiddo. For that price, I'd rather you get yourself a piano. I miss your playing. Anyway, Miko has decided that I am to learn Japanese cooking. I start tomorrow. I can't understand a thing, but figured as long as I follow what she is doing, I can't go wrong. The ingredients look very simple. Shinji says everything has these 4 ingredients: dashi, soya sauce, mirin, rice vinegar. Just put them in any combination and you're guaranteed to make something taste Japanese.

Miko saved you this rice cake. She finally got hold of some sugar and she and Shinji went nuts over it. I still prefer chocolate.

Good night. Wake me up to say goodbye before you leave for work.

Mom.

The dinner table was littered with little misshapen origami animals. Glenda must have waited up for her and was the last to go to bed. If it had been Miko or Shinji, they always very scrupulously left the downstairs lights on for her, "just in case you step on a centipede or a rat". Glenda always turned off all the lights out of habit. The house was left pitch dark. The steps creaked as Kate went upstairs.

It was a humid summer night of roaring cicadas. She was dying for a bath, but didn't want to wake everyone up with the sound of running taps. She could hear Glenda snoring as she crept past the first bedroom. Miko's deep breathing in the second. She went past the little upstairs foyer where they kept the sofa, newspapers and boxes of books. Shinji occupied the smallest room at the back of the house. Glenda said he kept his cigarettes (if he had any) in a small chest of drawers, bottom drawer, under the socks. The chest was just beside the door.

Kate slid open the paper screen door of his bedroom. There were no locks on any doors in this type of house. She crept inside and opened the drawer noiselessly, two packs of cigarettes in her hand.

Bam! She was shoved to the ground, her arm twisted behind her back. It hurt. She learned self-defense. She struggled free and struck him; he caught her and rolled. They slammed against the sliding window, it shivered open and let in a sliver of moonlight.

Bam! Crack!

Shiiiinng!

A slender dagger appeared. She gasped and grabbed his hand. He tripped her; she fell, sprawling, then lashed out at his legs. He fell.

"Shinji!" she gasped. "It's me!"

"So *you're* the one stealing my cigarettes!" he shouted. He pushed her so that she fell back down on the tatami mat. "You! You've taken everything, now you want to take even the small things! You have no shame!" He slapped her.

"Aw! How dare you!" she slapped him back. It caught him completely by surprise.

He tightened his grip on her and sat on her so that she could not move.

"It's not me, it's my Mom!" she howled.

"You're a liar!" he retorted. "Glenda-san does not smoke! I saw you open my drawer!"

"Get off me, I can't breathe," she said, tugging at his yukata. He was surprisingly strong. "Turn on the lights. Look in there, I returned two packs to you. I swear to God. I was hoping you wouldn't notice Mom had taken them."

Still holding on to her with one hand, he jerked open the drawer with the other. *Krunk!* He reached to feel inside it.

"Got them from the embassy tonight. For you."

His grip on her slackened.

"Now do you believe me?"

"Why does she have to steal my cigarettes?" he glared. "Do you know how expensive they are for me to buy from the black market? *She* can get all the cigarettes she wants, it's not as if *you* can't afford them!"

"She's not allowed to smoke. The doctor said. That's why she had to steal. I'm sorry."

He turned on the lights. By now, their mothers were at his bedroom door. Still in their sleep clothes, they held on to each other, rumpled and speechless with shock. Miko began scolding him in Japanese. He got off Kate and re-arranged his crumpled yukata; re-tied his belt.

Glenda's mouth was still agape. "Is that a real samurai knife?"

"That's it. I'm confiscating this weapon," said Kate, rising to her feet. She held out her hand. "Give it to me."

He scowled, handing it over. "I have an even bigger one."

Kate smacked his arm; he hit her back. She punched him. He tripped her. Another scuffle. They sprawled on the futon, trading blows.

Glenda and Miko yelled out in a mix of English and Japanese and finally pried them apart.

"I'll teach him to hit a woman!" cried Kate angrily, nursing her cheek.

"I'll teach her to hit a citizen of Japan!" retorted Shinji, his nose bloodied.

Miko wedged herself between the two of them, imploring in Japanese.

"Lord Almighty." Glenda panted. "And they were worried about *me* not getting along with the Orientals."

❀

It was Sunday morning. Kate and her mother decided to skip church.

"*Hai, ano, ne, sumimasen, chotto,*" said Glenda at the kitchen table. Miko was inspecting the Japanese soup that Glenda had put together. The stove bubbled away softly. "*Hai, ano, ne, sumimasen, chotto.*"

Miko corrected her pronunciation patiently.

"Hey kiddo," Glenda called out to the tiny strip of graveled yard beyond the kitchen door. "Apparently, if I can just say these five words really convincingly, I can shop for groceries at the market with Miko, or just about go anywhere in Japan on my own, no problem. You just say them properly, confidently, and – get this – you can say them in any order, and they'd still work. Right, Shinji?"

Shinji did not reply. He was sitting on the steps, smoking in the yard.

Kate sat beside him. Each looked in a different direction, deliberately avoiding each other's gaze.

"Right, Shinji?" hollered Glenda again, with forced cheer. Kate and Shinji had been giving each other the silent treatment the entire weekend, ever since the incident of the cigarettes. Despite Miko's intervention, Shinji had not forgiven Glenda and her daughter. "That's what you told me, right, Shinji-sensei? You better be right."

Miko went out into the yard, looked at Kate and Shinji, shook her head with a sigh, and began pinning up the wet laundry. Shinji rose to his feet and tried to help her; she pushed him away impatiently.

He scowled, returned the cigarette to his lips and sat down beside Kate.

"*Chotto, sumimasen! Ano, ne, hai!*"

Miko looked up from her laundry, distressed, "Glenda-san!"

"*Ne! Ano!*"

Miko said something to Shinji and prodded him with her foot. He refused to budge. Exasperated, Miko went indoors to correct Glenda.

"Hey Shinji," came Glenda's raspy voice. "What am I doing wrong? Your mom's busting my chops."

Kate said, looking at the cloudless sky, "She's probably trying to tell you that Shinji is full of shit, and that you can't just scramble the order. The words aren't all interchangeable. I mean, think about it, Mom. Would what he said make sense in English?"

Silence. Then, Glenda grumbled, "I knew it was too good to be true. This is tougher than French. At least French is in alphabets. This is all so squiggly. *Gu-ren-da. Gu-ren-da.* Hey, look, I can write my own name! Pretty soon I can be a translator at your office, kiddo! Or a Japanese cook. You guys need to employ a cook? I'm making sushi tonight."

A soft noise from Shinji.

Kate darted a look at him. He was trying not to laugh. She reached for the cigarette he was raising to his lips and wrenched it away from him.

He opened his mouth to protest. She raised her finger to her lips, indicating her mother.

Then, still staring at him, Kate brought his cigarette to her mouth and very deliberately drew a deep, luxurious drag.

Shinji narrowed his eyes at her.

She blew the smoke out carelessly, then raised her eyebrows at him in a challenge.

He scowled, reached into his pocket, and

promptly lit another cigarette.

They smoked in the sunny courtyard in silence, each facing a different direction.

"Hai, chotto, ano, ne, sumimasen. Sumimasen, ne, ano, chotto, hai."

❁

"Shinji! Shinji! *Hayaku*!"

He dropped his parcels and ran into the house. His mother was in a complete panic.

Kate lay writhing on the floor.

"What happened?" he asked.

Glenda said, "I don't know! I asked her to try my sushi!"

Shinji looked at the dinner table. He scanned the dishes, then grabbed a small bottle of soy sauce. "This is *shoyu*! Not *tamari*! I did not buy this!"

"*I* bought it," said Glenda. "I was out with your mom – it's just soy sauce!"

Kate stopped moving. She had lost consciousness.

Shinji lifted her in his arms. Then he turned to Glenda, almost savagely, "Only buy *tamari* in this house! *Tamari* is soy sauce with no wheat! Other types of soy sauce have wheat!"

"But they look the same!" cried Glenda. "They're all soy sauce! Isn't soy sauce made from soy?"

Miko ransacked the place trying to find Kate's adrenalin kit.

Shinji hurried out of the house carrying Kate. "I

have one in the car!"

They ran out of the yard into the darkening lane. Neighbors coming home from their evening errands stopped short in astonishment. A dog began barking excitedly. A single yellow street lamp illuminated the car.

"Open it!" cried Shinji to Glenda. "Take my keys!" He threw them at her. "Quick!"

Shinji commanded his mother in quick-fire Japanese. Glenda watched helplessly. A small crowd had gathered. Miko drew the kit out of the glove box. Shinji lowered Kate gently into the back seat. Miko tore open the kit and filled the syringe with steady hands. Her son grabbed it from her.

"*Doko?*" cried Shinji.

"*Koko!*" She pulled up Kate's woolen skirt.

He stabbed her in the thigh; threw away the empty syringe. "Kate." He crawled into the backseat with her and lifted her head. "Kate."

"I've killed her," sobbed Glenda. "My only child. I'm a stupid old woman."

"Kate," said Shinji.

"I had always been so careful — ever since she was a baby," sobbed Glenda. "I always checked. I always asked. I had a perfect record. I got careless in Japan. How am I supposed to know? Damn you people! Why did we come to this goddamned country! We should have just let you all rot!"

Miko put her arms around Glenda.

"Kate," said Shinji, putting his hand on her forehead, pushing aside her hair, feeling her neck for her pulse. "Come on, Kate."

A bevy of male and female voices from the crowd shouted excited suggestions in Japanese, but he ignored them.

He shut his eyes and leaned his forehead against hers. "*Ikanaide.*"

She opened her eyes and frowned. "What?"

"She's all right!" cried Shinji.

Relieved, the crowd began to disperse. The show was over.

"My throat's swelled up." She took a deep, sobbing breath.

Glenda peered into the car, her face tear-stained. "The soy sauce had wheat in it. I almost killed you, kiddo."

Shinji made her sit up. Her face was red and her eyes, streaming. She looked down at his arms firmly wrapped around her. "Go away."

He did not let go.

"Go away!" She struggled. "I'm going to heave."

Shinji held her as she threw up on the sidewalk.

Miko wiped her with her apron.

"This is a new low," said Kate, sniffing. She managed a smile at Shinji. "Least I didn't do it in the car. Belongs to the government of Japan."

"You fell down. Look at your head. There is a bump." He touched her forehead. "Come. Let's go inside."

Kate ignored him, raising her arms and staring at the blotchy hives growing on her skin. "Wow."

"Let's get her to the hospital," said Glenda.

"The hospital!" said Shinji with distaste. "Have you seen our hospitals? No. I'll bring the doctor here. If it's Kate-san, they will come."

"Don't carry me, Shinji," said Kate.

"Oh for God's sake, let him carry you!" barked Glenda. "You'd be dead if it weren't for Shinji! I couldn't find your kit! Luckily he always kept a spare in the car!"

"I'm too heavy," said Kate.

"Shut up," said Shinji, lifting her.

"Shut up?" she repeated. "Is that how you talk to your boss?"

"You're not so strong, and I'm not so weak," he replied, and carried her into the house.

❀

She could hear every loud conversation, every creak and sigh of the wooden house on a still afternoon. Since Shinji did not have to drive her to work, he spent the morning in the kitchen teaching Glenda Japanese script. She must devote the afternoon, he declared, to 'self study'. Ink was expensive. She practiced with a wet inkbrush on newspaper while chanting each syllable out loud.

A, i, u, e, o. あいうえお

Ka, ki, ku, ke, ko. かきくけこ

Kate had been in bed all day. The doctor had come and gone. He was one of the new army doctors, a fresh graduate. They talked about Yale and Harvard.

Shinji arrived outside her door but did not enter. "*Shitsureishimasu!*" he said sulkily.

"Yeah."

Ssshhaaack! The door slid back.

Shinji brought a lunch tray. "Newman-sensei said he will come again tomorrow to check on you."

"What! I'm totally fine. What a waste of army medical resources."

"I agree. But when men are in love they stop at nothing."

"In love?"

"That is the only reason why he is here," he declared. "No medical reason at all. Newman-sensei is the handsomest of all the American doctors. The Japanese staff at your office said so. He is very tall. Plus, he speaks very good Japanese. He has already broken many Japanese girls' hearts. But he prefers his own kind. They told me he admires you greatly, thinks you are one of the cleverest women he has ever met, and vows to marry you by autumn."

Kate gave him a distrustful look. "Is this all really true?

"Um! That's what the ladies say at your office," said Shinji solemnly, pouring soup from a flask into a wooden bowl. "Naturally, I am very concerned."

She sat up in bed and ate, ignoring him.

"I would lose my position as the sole man in the house," he continued. He was kneeling on the tatami. Now he placed his hands firmly on his knees and leaned forward with an air of tragic disclosure. "Kate-san does not know this, but position in Japanese society is very important for a man. I already work for a foreigner. Worse, a foreign woman. I have lost my position in the community. But at least, I am the head of this house. Imagine if I have to lose my place to Newman-sensei. A Japanese household cannot have two leaders. One must go."

His speech finished, he bowed his head in regret and lowered his long lashes.

"Very good, Shinji," said Kate, picking up her chopsticks. "Now, go take a pen and write that all down. You have the beginnings of a great postwar Japanese novel."

He chuckled. It was all clearly an act.

"Shinji, shut the door please," said Kate.

He turned to go.

"No, stay here, *and* shut the door."

A shadow crossed his face.

"I'm not going to eat you."

He slid the door shut carefully and knelt back down. On his off days, he wore his yukata woven with indigo-blue and golden-brown stripes. It kept him cooler in the summer than his starchy Western suit. He had only one yukata, which he bought with his first paycheck. His mother kept it scrupulously clean and ironed. Kate loved the pattern, the look of it on him. If she had a choice, she would want him to never wear Western clothes.

"You needn't worry about losing your job," she said in a low voice. "Even if I leave, you'll get to stay here. I'll make sure of it."

"Kate-san, it was a joke," he said, grinning. "I

was trying to cheer you up."

"It's your house, isn't it?"

His smile faded.

She pushed the tray aside and leaned forward on her futon. She reached for his left hand.

"Kate-san!" He put his hands behind his back.

❀

Downstairs, Miko looked up from the laundry.

"Don't worry," said Glenda calmly, dipping her ink brush in a dish of water. "He has a samurai sword."

❀

"I can't touch your hands?"

"Hands are private."

"Very well. *May* I touch your hands, Shinji?"

She felt his fingertips with hers gently. He said nothing, a haunted look in his eyes.

"The calluses should have been gone by now," said Kate softly. She held up his hand and examined the long, slender fingers. "You play secretly. Somewhere, where we do not hear."

He shook his head slowly.

"Where is your violin?"

Silence.

She touched the tips of his fingers to her lips. She kissed each fingertip lightly. "Dear Shinji. You are the son of the music professor who once lived here,

Tadao Nakamura. Where were you during the war? You disappeared without a trace. When they came to conscript you, there was no son to be found. Instead, the Nakamura household only had a daughter, a musician who travelled with her mother and other middle-aged women singers to entertain at seaside resorts."

He pulled his hand away abruptly.

"The Nakamura family originally had four members," said Kate. "Professor Nakamura, his wife Miko, his son, Shinji, and his daughter, Yuki. I traced you all to the seaside town of K ------, December, 1938. Then I lost you."

"I did not want to be found," he said finally. "My country was trying to murder me."

"You escaped the draft?"

He said nothing.

"You never had a medical condition, did you?"

He refused to answer, his head bowed.

"What happened to your father and sister?" Kate folded herself against the floor. She peered at his lowered face. "Shinji. I'm not asking as a member of the US government. I'm asking because I care about you. How can I live in this house, every day, knowing that it is your house?"

He drew in a breath deeply and looked stubborn.

"Fine," said Kate, resigned. She sat up. "You are entitled to your secrets. I shouldn't have asked. I won't tell Mom anything. She suspects something – but – all right? It's between us. You may go."

Shinji did not move. They sat in silence for nearly five whole minutes. Downstairs, Miko scrubbed tiles vigorously with a wire brush. Next door, a neighbor aired out her futons and beat them free of dust.

Pom, pom, pom.

Pom, pom, pom.

"In the car."

Kate raised her eyebrow.

"My violin is in the car. When I am bored, I practice while waiting for you outside the office."

"I never hear you."

"There is no bow. I do not want anyone else to hear."

"I see."

"My father was a violinist. During the war, he became very ill. That was why we went to the seaside. There was not enough food or medicine in Kyoto. We went to Nagoya, but there was nothing there either. We did not even bother to try Tokyo. Finally, we went to the seaside town to find my aunt, but she was sick herself. She died soon after we arrived. Then my father died. Then my younger sister, Yuki, became sick." His eyes burned. "Do you know how it feels, to see them dying, one by one, in front of you? You think you know what it is like. You complain about it every day in the car. But for me, it was worse. They were my own family. There was nothing I could do. There was no doctor, no medicine, nobody to help. Everyone was in the same situation, town after town. Meanwhile the army was coming and taking the boys." His voice sank.

"To be *kamikaze* pilots?"

"No. Those were still early days. We were going to China. To replace those who never came back."

Kate eyed him steadily.

He raised his face. "It's not *cammy-katzy*. You all say it wrong."

"Why does it matter? It's a horrible word."

"*Kami kaze*," he pronounced it in the proper Japanese way. "It's not one word. It's two. Two separate, beautiful words."

"No," said Kate, shaking her head. "Don't think I don't know what it was all about. Fourteen year-old boys, brainwashed, put in junk planes – retired planes that didn't even work properly – so that they could crash themselves into our ships. Stupid, stupid."

"But it's not the fault of the words."

"I beg your pardon?"

"It's not the fault of the words," he repeated stubbornly. "Do you know what the words mean?"

"Yeah," snapped Kate. "*Kamikaze*. 'Divine Wind'. A force of nature sent to exterminate us! It's sick."

Shinji shook his head. "Kate-san is the master of words at the office, but she is scared of *kami kaze*."

"I'm not scared, I just don't have to like it."

He made a scissoring motion with his fingers. "Kate-san, separate the two words. Cut. They become different. For thousands of years the words were used in poetry, in prayers. We use the words even now, every day. *Kami* is God. It is the power that you feel around you in a mountain forest. It is the empty heart of the shrine. Even saying the word, *kami,* creates a feeling of wonder, of being watched and protected by something big, a giant. It is scary, but safe. *Kaze* is wind. *Kaze* can be a typhoon that destroys a village, or a gentle spring breeze on your face. But now, because of the war, *kami kaze*, two beautiful ideas put together, has become one dirty word. Now, to the whole world, it just means a suicidal war tactic, involving mad people. *Cammy-katzy.* Sometimes I hear Americans on the radio using it like a joke word, to mean someone is crazy or obsessed. It's so unfair. That's not what it meant originally."

She studied him. Then she shook her head in exasperation. "I'm sorry, but it's too late in the day to try to rehabilitate the word *kamikaze.* Hearing that word is like hearing fingernails across a chalkboard for all Americans."

"It sounds like noise to you because you don't understand Japanese. But for me, I can hear the meaning. Both meanings – the American meaning, and the Japanese meaning – at the same time. It's very painful."

"Shinji. I'm from San Francisco. When you guys bombed Pearl Harbor, we thought we were next," said Kate. There was steel in her voice. "We rounded up the Japanese families in my neighborhood and put them in internment camps. Children, pets, everything. They appealed, put an ad in the local paper, saying they were Americans, but we didn't even listen. The anti-submarine nets we built stretched seven miles long across San Francisco Bay. If we could build a wall to keep you out, we would have. You can't change *kamikaze*. It's poison. Forever."

"You yourself said it's not the thing itself that is poisonous. It's people that are poisonous."

"When did I say that?"

"You said that about wheat."

She sighed.

"All humans fear death. Suicide is the loneliest thing that could happen to a human being. Even if you believe your death is a worthy sacrifice – how you must suffer to think it! They say that some pilots did not want to die. They were forced to do it. They would be killed if they didn't. They say that the pilots were injected with drugs that made them lose their mind. Do you believe this?"

"Don't be naïve."

"I don't know if it's true. I don't know if people can really find out the truth. All I know is, Americans think that we were all devoted to the Emperor and signed up to be *kamikaze* pilots. They are wrong. In reality, so many of us refused! Nobody ever talks about this, but it is true! We did not believe in the propaganda. We all heard horror stories. Boys my age, they tried all kinds of things – bribing people, running away, hiding in the mountains. My parents tried to protect me, but when my father died, we ran out of options. Do you really want to know what happened?"

She nodded.

"Can you keep it to yourself?"

She nodded again.

He reached inside his clothes and pulled out something he wore around his neck. A little cloth bundle. She had noticed it before and assumed it was one of those religious amulets that they sold everywhere. He began untying it. The knot was tight. "I have never shown anyone this letter. Only my mother and I know. She swore me to secrecy. Even now, she's afraid. But it's already four years after the war. If I don't tell someone, I will burst. What is the worst that could happen? I don't think it is a crime under any American law, is it, Kate-san?"

"Depends on what it is," said Kate quietly.

"My sister Yuki was a year younger than me. We both played the violin. My father had lived in England as a student. The Japanese government sponsored him to study at the Royal Academy of Music. In London, he had an old landlady who liked him very much. She and her husband took care of him like a son. He ended up living and teaching there for many years. During the first World War, he refused to come back to Japan. When the war ended, his parents begged him to return. They had arranged a marriage for him. By that time, he was already 38, and my mother 25. In 1920, I was born. He gave up returning to England. Yuki and I were both raised to play the violin. He made us learn English. He dreamed of sending us overseas, but my mother always refused to let us go. She would miss us too much, she said. So we never applied for any scholarships and stayed close to her.

"Whenever Yuki and I used to perform together, people said we looked like a pair of sisters. I used to hate them saying that I looked like Yuki. I would get into fights, learned to protect myself from bullies. My father died in the winter of 1938. By the sea. We had no medicine for Yuki's fever. We were running out of food. Our only hope was to split up. I would join the army. Yuki and my mother planned to join a group of women singers we had seen play at the resort. If we didn't split up, we would all starve to death. But I was against the idea. I was sure I would never see them again if I was sent to China. I argued and argued. I said I would find a better way, that I would take care of us all. One night, during a storm, I woke up and found that Yuki had disappeared. She had left her clothes and shoes. And this letter."

He put in her hand a worn, scrolled scrap of paper. She unrolled it and saw tiny strings of squiggly Japanese handwriting, written in vertical columns. It looked like poetry.

Shinji had it memorized by now. "'My beloved Shinji, I am very sick. There is no point feeding the last food we have to a dying person. Wear my clothes and take my name. Tell the army that Shinji died. There is no other option. Mother is now in your hands. You must do everything in your power to live. You must fulfill Father's dream. Your sister, Yuki.'"

He stared at the floor. "I went out to find her. I

only had a lantern with a candle in it. It was impossible in the storm. In the morning, the sea was very calm."

❀

"Thirteen meters."

"How many feet is that?"

"Forty," said Kate nervously.

Newman and the new contingent of army doctors filled up her office. They had heard the news.

One of them looked up from his math. "Actually thirteen meters is 42.65 feet."

"You're not making me feel better," said Kate.

"Let me get this straight," said Newman. "If you jump off this balcony, your wish will come true?"

"Supposedly," said Kate. "All I'm concerned about is the dramatic effect. This stalemate is in need of a big, bold move from our side. I'm willing to stake my career on it. I have the support of Tokyo. They are out of ideas."

The young men burst into excited discussion. They were the brightest lads from the country's best schools. Their accents covered every part of the States: Midwest, South, East, West.

"Whoa, I gotta try this!" "Doesn't seem that hard. It's only three stories." "Can you make more than one wish per jump?" "Is there a prescribed way of jumping?" "Yeah, head first or feet first?" "Is it the jump that creates the magic, or the fact that you landed and didn't die?" "Can you die from a forty-foot jump?" "Depends on what you land on." "If there is a strong forest canopy cover, the branches might break your fall." "Let's go check it out. I'll drive!" "I wanna go!"

"We'll need more than one jeep," Newman turned to Kate. "Are you sure it's thirteen meters exactly?"

The men smoothed their hair back, jammed on their hats. "Let's go measure the sucker." "Yeah. At that height, even the difference of half a foot could mean the difference between brain damage or no brain damage." "That's why I would recommend we jump feet first." "If there is a slope, you could break your fall by rolling. I always roll when I fall off during polo." "If we wore helmets - "

"STOP!" yelled Kate, tapping her desk with a ruler. "My God, you're like a bunch of freshmen."

The doctors settled down.

"NOBODY is doing the jump except me," said Kate. "I already said."

Murmurs of discontentment.

"Hey, Schroeder, we respect you an'all," said a Texan surgeon ruefully. "But no way in hell are we gonna let a woman take a hit for the team."

"Yeah."

"It stinks any way you look at it," said the Texan.

"Hear, hear!"

"Oh, don't pull the 'woman' thing on me!" said Kate. "You're worse than the GIs."

"With all due respect, ma'am," said another medic, sitting on her desk. She pointed her ruler at him; he got up hastily. "You're a civilian, and a woman, and we're all officers. We should take the risk. If you don't let us all go, we'll draw lots among us and nominate one guy to substitute for you."

"I'm the head of the department, aren't I?" said Kate, rising to her feet. "We caused the public health crisis. I am the chief, I have to personally apologize. That's the Japanese way. If I do it at Kiyomizudera, in front of the Japanese people, with all the reporters there, if I play my cards right, it might just work."

"That's insane, man."

"You are one crazy lady."

Newman grinned broadly. "You know who was her old man? Harry Schroeder."

"The photographer?"

"Wow."

"The man ran into battle without a gun in his hands, towards enemy fire, so he could take a better picture," said Newman. "A forty foot jump is nothing."

More heated discussion. Not only did they want to protect a woman, they coveted the danger. They were going to steal her idea. She rose at her desk, ready for battle.

A knock on the door.

Her Japanese staff filed in, bowing.

"Kate-san," said her Japanese secretary. "The engineers are here. It's very important."

Kate was astonished as more people pushed into the already-crammed room.

"Good morning, Schroeder-san," said the head of

a local construction company. He worked with the US army engineers on building bridges and repairing roads. He shook her hand. "I am Chief Engineer Takahashi Jiro. We have a design that we hope Schroeder-san will approve."

A blueprint was unrolled at her desk.

"This was jointly designed by us and our American colleagues," he said. He hooked his thumbs on his suspenders proudly. "For many years, Kyoto people knew there was a simple solution to the problem, but nobody wanted to be the first to suggest it. We believe that now is the time. After all, it is a new era. According to our calculations, a fall from the *butai* of Kiyomizudera will be perfectly broken by an inflatable balloon exactly 1.8 meters high. We have air pumps that can keep the balloon at just the right density – see?"

Everyone crowded round to look. It was an artist's rendition of a giant cushion on the slope of Mount Otowa, right below the famous balcony. It included a string of neatly-written formulas calculating the impact force from falling objects of different weights.

"It is the perfect combination of science and tradition," said the chief engineer. "We are supported by the authority of an old Kyoto legend. Ever since the temple was first built, so many pilgrims died when attempting the jump. The legend says, one day, a giant spider will come down from Mount Otowa, crawl under the *butai*, and spin a huge balloon made of silk. Everyone would be safe, forever after. As far as we know, nobody had ever made this balloon. But now we have the technology. Imported from America."

The Texan doctor drawled, "Amen and thank you for saving us from ourselves."

"Let me get this straight," said Kate suspiciously. "Isn't it cheating? If we cushion my fall, it doesn't invalidate the whole process?"

"No. The important thing is to have the faith to look over the terrifying edge and jump off," said the chief engineer. "It's the courage to leap that matters, not how you end up."

"Doesn't sound right," said Kate.

"It's true, it's true," said the chief engineer, nodding solemnly. "The famous *butai* jump has had many interpretations throughout the centuries. Ours is at least as correct as everyone else's version."

"Take it at face value, Schroeder," said Newman, admiring the blueprint. "At the very least, you could pitch it as an unprecedented case of US-Japan collaboration on solving an ancient problem. You're gonna be on the cover of LIFE magazine."

❧

DEAR _____,

Kate's fingers flew over the typewriter keyboard. *Clack-clack-clack!*

THANK YOU VERY MUCH FOR INVITING ME TO

_____ *ON* _____.

I REGRET THAT I CANNOT ATTEND DUE TO

*WORK COMMITMENTS. PLEASE ACCEPT MY WARMEST
REGARDS AND THE ENCLOSED GIFT.*
SINCERELY YOURS,
K.A. SCHROEDER

Zzzhupp! She pulled out the sheet and handed it to her Japanese secretary. "You can reply to all of them this way. I'll sign them. Please decide on the gift for me. I trust you."

"Yes, Kate-san," said the woman. She studied the note carefully. "'Due to work commitments.' Can I personally use this style of expression to say no to an American party?"

"You? Sure."

The secretary said modestly, "I am invited to a lot of parties by the American soldiers. I want to say no."

Kate smiled. Her secretary spoke excellent English, was only twenty years old, and very pretty. "If you don't want to go, just tell them to buzz off."

"They are always inviting the unmarried girls. I only go if Newman-sensei asks. He is very popular. Do you think Newman-sensei is good-looking?"

Kate made a face. "No."

"No? We think he looks like Randolph Scott!"

"Ugh! No! I think he looks like…Charlie Chaplin."

"Ha ha ha!"

"Listen, you don't have to accept every invitation to a party. Doesn't matter who the guy is."

Her secretary's eyes grew large. "Even if it's General MacArthur?"

Kate relented. "Oh, *I* would go if it's MacArthur, but - "

"Ha ha ha!"

"Seriously, you don't have to give a reason. Just say no."

"*Wakarimashita,* Kate-san."

"If you have any problems, you tell me. I can make annoying people disappear. All I have to do is sign a piece of paper."

"Ha ha ha!"

"All right, let's get out of here, I'm starving."

They got up, put on their hats, slung their handbags over their arms. They had stayed late to finish up a mass mailing.

"Actually, I like American parties," said the secretary, turning off the lights. "But if I go too many times, my parents worry that I would be known as a girl who goes with the American soldiers. It would affect my ability to get a good husband next time."

"Hell, we wouldn't want that," said Kate in good humor.

"I was a bit frightened of working in this office for American men. But I am very happy to work for Kate-san. My parents are very happy too."

"That's right, you girls are safe with me," said Kate. She reached into her pile of mail and pulled out a long cardboard box from her packages. It was very light and was marked FRAGILE. "But the men of Japan, they better watch out."

Their laughter rang out in the corridor.

❀

Shinji drove up to the construction site.

"Oh…my…God," said Kate, stepping out of the car.

Men, stripped to the waist in the hot weather, busied about directing cranes. Little Japanese and American flags fluttered around the job site. The giant red balloon sat on a wooden platform. It was still flat, but it was clear that when inflated, it would be quite impressive.

"This is not very efficient," said Shinji. "It is a waste of silk at a time like this."

"It's beautiful, though."

"They are just doing it for the news cameras."

"Well, it *is* propaganda."

"This is stupid. You should have checked with me before giving your approval." Shinji looked at Kate pointedly. "Everyone knows that in modern day Japan, it is not necessary to take the old custom literally. I was just joking when I mentioned it, but you took me seriously."

"What the hell do you mean?"

"It is not necessary to physically make the jump."

She stared.

"Nowadays, all you have to do to show your faith is to stand over the scary part, look down, and just *imagine* yourself making the jump. That is sufficient."

"What!"

"The temple authorities officially decreed this back in the 1910s. It is now the official rule. The leap of faith is not meant to be taken literally. Otherwise we would have too many reckless deaths."

She whistled. "Now you tell me."

❀

Miko and Glenda sat side by side on the wooden ledge facing the courtyard. They were both wearing Japanese cotton housekeeping smocks; their heads wrapped in large, brightly printed handkerchiefs. They had worn themselves out washing all the futons in the house. The white, padded layers were now draped over the balcony, drying in the sun.

Glenda turned the leaves of a tattered women's magazine. *VOGUE*. It was a year out of date. She had scrounged it off some American woman she had met at the market.

Glenda turned the page. Miko gasped. A lavish two-page spread. Charles James' 1948 collection. A ballroom of pale ladies in pastel silks, poised like Greek goddesses. A triumph in post-war fashion.

"Hm…this one. You should get this one. I think you'd look really good in it," said Glenda, pointing.

Miko smiled and considered the outfit Glenda picked. Right now, it was difficult to imagine that world.

"Which one do you think I should get?" asked Glenda.

Miko pointed to a pale green confection.

"Yeah! I'm partial to green. I had red hair. If I wear that, I'm definitely dying my hair."

Miko looked at Glenda fondly. "Glenda-san."

"Yeah."

She said in halting English, "Please take care of Shinji."

Glenda grinned. "Me? Take care of him? More likely it'll be the other way around. Where are you going?"

Miko made a characteristic, polite noise and shook her head. She struggled to say something; a feeling of perplexed happiness came to her eyes; then she made a long, complicated, eloquent speech in Japanese to Glenda. Shinji was not at home to translate. But Glenda was not perturbed. She patted Miko's hand and nodded. No translation was needed.

❀

Ting!

It was a windchime, spinning in the summer breeze.

Kate stood on the grand balcony of the Shrine of Clear Waters. It was appropriately called a *butai* 舞台, a theater stage from which she would give a compelling performance in a last-ditch attempt to heal relations between the army medical corps and a distrustful and beleaguered populace.

Ting!

Far away, a housekeeper polished the old wood of a staircase in a house she had once owned.

A Japanese violinist in England reluctantly packed for home.

A girl left her clothes behind in a neat pile and walked into the sea.

A boy lived as a girl through the darkest years of the war, playing the violin with a group of travelling musicians from resort town to resort town, fearing at every stop that his past would catch up with him. Long after the war was over, the boy – now a man – sat alone in a black car. Under his chin, a violin, cushioned against his pale skin with a crisp white handkerchief to prevent the telltale mark. He fingered the strings without a bow and made no sound.

Ting-ting!

She thought of all the massive forces in world history that conspired to bring Shinji and her together this golden afternoon, before the news cameras and the brightly-attired crowd of Kyoto citizens and their American occupiers.

Below the terrace, a giant red silk balloon shimmered in the breeze. It sat on a platform, above the actual graves of past pilgrims who had not survived the fall.

Kate unfolded a paper. Shinji stood next to her as her translator. To the audience's surprise, Kate began reading her speech confidently in Japanese. It was written out for her in romanized script, translated by Shinji and further vetted by two official Japanese translators. With her permission, her original draft had been cut into half by her Japanese aides, then cut into half again. What was left was short, powerful. To be sincere in apology, it is important to show, but not show too much. And what little she did show had to be perfect. At home, he had made her practice, over and over again, as he sat with his back turned, his eyes closed, correcting her. "It is important to say it like a woman," he had said. "The Japanese people, they are used to seeing America as a big, rough, foreign soldier. This will surprise them, make them listen. Use only the most polite and feminine of expressions. Your tone must rise and fall. You must become a completely different person." Her paper was penciled all over with notations in both their handwriting, like a music score.

When she finished, Shinji read the English translation of her speech for the American audience present. Kate then asked everyone to observe a minute's silence for the infants who died. They clasped their palms and lowered their heads.

Kate wore a plain, white kimono with a white belt, a maiden to be sacrificed, a figure from the picture scrolls of old. Her long, brown hair was loose in the wind. She had never felt more feminine in her life.

She thought, then, of the mantra of her adult life.

I am not that weak. You are not that strong.

She had proved this theory, over and over again, as a woman to the men around her, and society had alternated between rewarding and chastising her for it. She was sure she was right.

Then, one day, a Japanese man with eyes like

dark caramel had come out and said, *You are not that strong. I am not that weak.*

And both beliefs were true.

Beside her, Shinji wore a formal black kimono with a white pom-pom tied in front. The crisp black silk was studded with five family crests. She was touched. He had gone to great lengths to find and borrow the suit for the occasion.

The mayor made a long, dull, ceremonial speech in Japanese. Kate said in a low voice, "You look quite dashing, Shinji."

"Thank you," he said curtly.

"How is the bow working out?"

"It is a good bow."

"So when can I hear you play?"

His tone was tolerant. "Just because Kate-san gave me a present of a good bow, does not mean I will play my violin for Kate-san."

"What! According to *Enjoy Your Time In Japan*, if I give a Japanese person a present, I create an obligation, and the Japanese person will give me a present back. Guaranteed."

"That is true," said Shinji haughtily. "But it is up to the Japanese recipient to decide what the return gift is."

"Have you decided?"

"The gift by a woman to a man of a violin bow is very unusual. Even confusing. Therefore, I am not sure of the customary return gift. I am still checking."

Kate laughed. "Well, at least you can take me out to a movie?"

He stared straight ahead, his nose in the air. "I shall continue to refuse your advances."

"Clearly you have surrendered! You even got dressed up today just for me."

"It is what Japanese men wear at funerals."

"Funerals," repeated Kate, narrowing her eyes. "Really."

He nodded calmly.

She cursed under her breath.

"Although, we also wear it at weddings." He bit his lip.

"The same kimono?"

"Yes, we only have one type."

"You are a sick race."

Shinji smiled, then looked regretful. "Ah. I forgot something. Too late now."

"What?"

"We should have tied your feet together," he said, looking down at her legs solemnly. "The women in the legends always do. For propriety. So that they would not be in disarray when their bodies are found."

"You're really enjoying this, aren't you?" she retorted.

"Of course!" A smile of genuine delight. "This is the most amazing thing Kyoto has ever seen! An American woman making a public apology in Japanese, and leaping off the Kiyomizudera *butai*. The national radio is here. Could you…make some sounds on your way down, so that the radio audience across Japan would have the full experience?"

"Sure you don't want to come with me?" she said sarcastically.

"No, no, that would deny the occasion of its spectacular meaning," he looked offended. "It's not a suicide pact of lovers. It is an apology, and also a chance for the United States to show its unshakeable faith, its moral fiber, and its ability to govern by example."

"Shinji-san, your English rhetoric is so good, you should be writing my speeches."

He inclined his head politely. "Kate-san is a good influence."

Applause. The mayor stepped off the platform and nodded to her.

Kate took a deep breath. "Let's do this, Shinji."

"*Ganbatte,* Kate."

Before the eyes of the watchful crowd, Kate walked the red carpet which had been ceremoniously strewn with flowers. She waved to her mother and Miko in the audience. She took a deep breath. She thought to look down just in case the balloon had accidentally deflated. She couldn't really see it in its entirety. It was screened by a thin canopy of fluttering leaves from a nearby tree.

It better be full of air. Better not be a leak.

She climbed over the balustrade. Her knees felt weak now. Three stories didn't seem much on the right side of the barrier. She had never jumped off a diving board before, let alone a building. It was clearly irrational. Every cell in her brain rebelled in protest.

Ting! Went the temple windchime, high above her from an unseen window.

Her faith must be strong, Shinji had said. Her wish, fervent. Her mind, clear. She thought only of beauty and redemption.

Kami. Kaze.

She leapt.

The crowd gasped.

Shinji hurried over to the edge with all the reporters and doctors in tow. He grabbed the balustrades. "Kate!" he yelled.

Glenda rasped, "Are you all right, kiddo?"

"Yo Schroeder!" yelled the army doctors. One by one they cupped their mouths and hollered into the glorious, green-gold view:

"Yo! Did you make it?"

"Talk to me, girlfriend!"

On the red balloon below, in a shower of fallen leaves, the white figure lay still. Silence in the hazy valley.

"SSSCHROOOOEEE-DER!" hollered the doctors.

Then, a tired cry. "Yeah, yeah."

Flashbulbs popped.

Congratulations and handshakes all around.

Forty feet below, Kate could hear the clapping and excited chatter. Soon, the engineers would be coming to get her. But for now, she floated alone on the buoyant, vast bubble of silk. The red fabric had been in the hot sun for hours and was pleasantly warm under her clothes. It was like lying on top of a freshly-baked custard pie.

The sky was cornflower blue and empty of clouds. She thought she was very big, but she had turned quite small in the arms of a vast, invisible, tender god. She felt very far from home. She had closed one door and opened another. There was no turning back now. This country would change her forever. And that was quite all right.

FIN

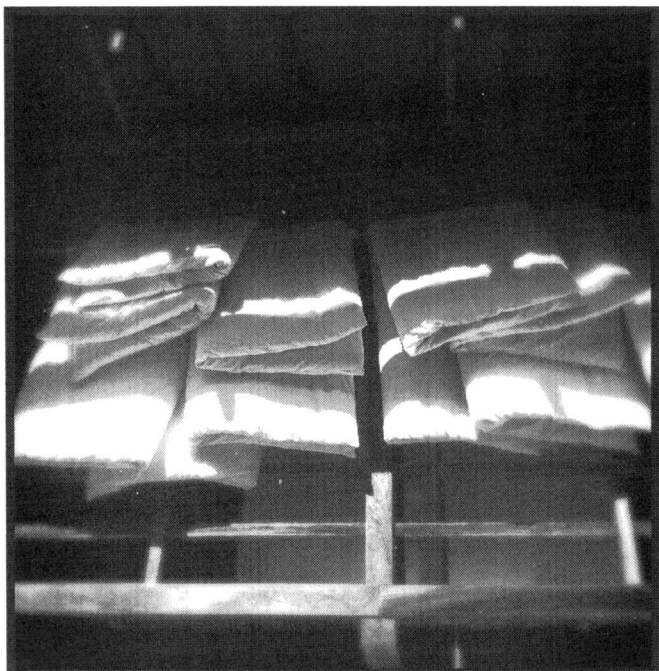

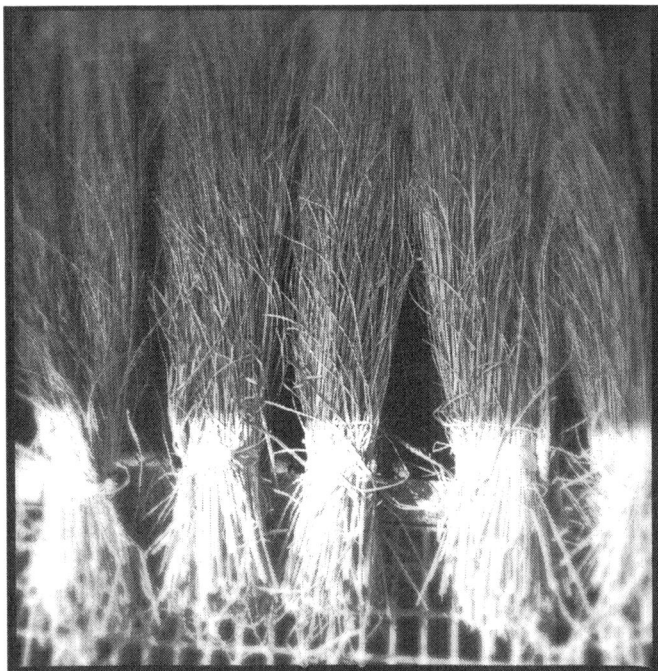

The photo/story 絵物語 is finished.

I don't want to make it any shorter or any longer.

Shut up, literary agent! I'm CHINESE.

Chinese people do not have "short stories" or "novels".

We have 小说 or 短篇小说.

Sometimes our poetry become plays, and our plays poetry.

We used to write on scrolls that could be cut off anywhere we pleased. We didn't even use punctuation so you wouldn't know when we stopped speaking

How long is a length of string?

Is it a rabbit? Or a rat?

(What else can I put in here to reach the
minimum pages necessary to put a title on
the spine of this book? ...)

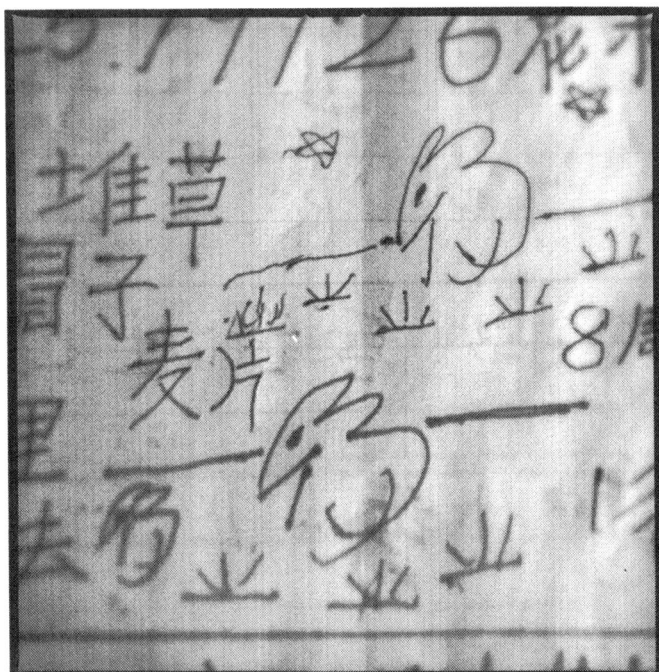

← A page from my 82 year-old grandma's notebook.

"Why are you drawing rabbits?" I ask.

"It's a rat," she says. "But you may think of it as a rabbit, if you wish."

END NOTES

My novels and short stories are living documents. In each, the goodwill of many people who helped in small but important ways. I am very grateful to my Chinese family in Singapore for allowing me to exploit their art and good humor, to Mandy in Hong Kong and Mizuyo-san in Japan, for their enthusiastic help with language, to Katy in Austin, for a sudden insight on violinists, and to Bailey, who specifically asked to be credited for "technical advice on all *gweilo* things."

This story – this entire story – was triggered by a single line in Charles Holcomb's *A History of East Asia*. I was in Singapore, suffering from jet-lag, reading books till dawn. At about four in the morning, I came across an arresting sentence of his. While laying out the historical facts of the Allied Occupation of postwar Japan, he added, as an aside, "Not a few participants in the occupation discovered a lifelong love and fascination for Japanese culture." A curt sentence, but what a tantalizing glimpse of untold stories! Immediately I saw Kate Schroeder typing away at her desk, coiffed in a 1940s manner. I began writing.

As my Singapore Chinese family was quick to point out, literature in English about WWII Asia is both stereotypical and depressing: they hoped I was not wasting time contributing to this dreary genre. I promised them that I would depart from the norm. Images of beefy GIs wooing 'geishas' in postwar Japan make me cringe. Historians have pointed out how victorious Americans (exemplified by MacArthur) imposed themselves on defeated Japan like a man imposing himself on a weak woman. It is time to update the narrative. What if the gender roles were reversed? What if the American 'victor' in question was a modern Californian career gal who finds herself confronting her Japanese counterpart? Shinji – sulky, complete with portable radio, Lucky Strikes, and a mysterious past – popped into my head. I had a story.

Writing historical fiction can be very limiting, which is why I usually write contemporary fiction. Researching this story (mostly after I wrote it) was quite educational, but still a bit of a drag. I did in fact stay in a wooden house near Kyoto with centipedes; and I do in fact, like Glenda, study the Japanese language; but the rest is all pure invention, sprinkled opportunistically with historical fact whenever it suited me. It is annoying to think that some smart aleck reader would write in or review this saying "you are an ignorant author, for the earthquake did not happen in winter, it was actually summer, and I happen to know because I was there at the time." In some parts I have deliberately chosen to depart from known facts in order to advance the story, or adhere to certain aesthetic preferences. These departures, hopefully, would not disturb your enjoyment of the story.

RECOMMENDED READING

There are innumerable WWII books covering America and Japan. Many are really boring. The following books may not all be relevant to this story, or to Occupied Japan, but I hope you will enjoy them after reading this book. I certainly did. To provide you with some context, the year following each title is approximately the year in which the work first appeared:

Holcomb, Charles, *A History of East Asia* (2011)

Dower, John W. *Embracing Defeat: Japan in the Wake of World War II* (1999)

Goto, Yumi, *Those Days in Muramatsu: One Woman's Memoir of Occupied Japan* (1996, reprinted 2014)

Smith, Kazuko, Makiko's Diary: *A Merchant Wife in 1910 Kyoto* (1981, reprinted 1995)

Ogasawara, Yuko, *Office Ladies and Salaried Men: Power, Gender, and Work in Japanese Companies* (1998)

Tanizaki, Junichiro, *In Praise of Shadows* (1933)

Kawabata, Yasunari, *Palm-of-the-Hand Stories* (1923-1972)

I am indebted to this author and his medical article, for bringing to light the 1948 diphtheria incident leading to the death of 68 infants, which really happened:

Nishimura, Sey, *Promoting Health During the American Occupation of Japan: The Public Health Section, Kyoto Military Government Team, 1945-1949,* which appeared in the *American Journal of Public Health* (2008).

thank you for reading!

x *Wena*

ABOUT THE AUTHOR

Wena Poon's novels and short stories have been professionally produced on the London stage, serialized as a *Book At Bedtime* on BBC Radio 4, and extensively anthologized and translated into French, Italian, and Chinese. She won the UK's Willesden Herald Prize for best short fiction. She was also nominated for Ireland's Frank O'Connor Award, France's *Prix Hemingway*, the Singapore Literature Prize, and the UK's Bridport Prize for Poetry. Her fiction is studied by British, American, Hong Kong and Singapore academics as examples of transnational literature. From 2011 through 2017, her short stories are studied by thousands of Singapore high school students sitting for the Cambridge 'O' Level Exams in Literature. She graduated *magna cum laude* in English Literature from Harvard and holds a J.D. from Harvard Law School. She is a lawyer by profession. www.wenapoon.com

スタジオウェナ

PUBLISHER	Sutajio Wena スタジオウェナ
TYPESET	Perpetua 13
PHOTOGRAPHY	iPhone 4 + Hipstamatic film

OTHER SUTAJIO WENA TITLES

スタジオウェナ の 本 カタログ

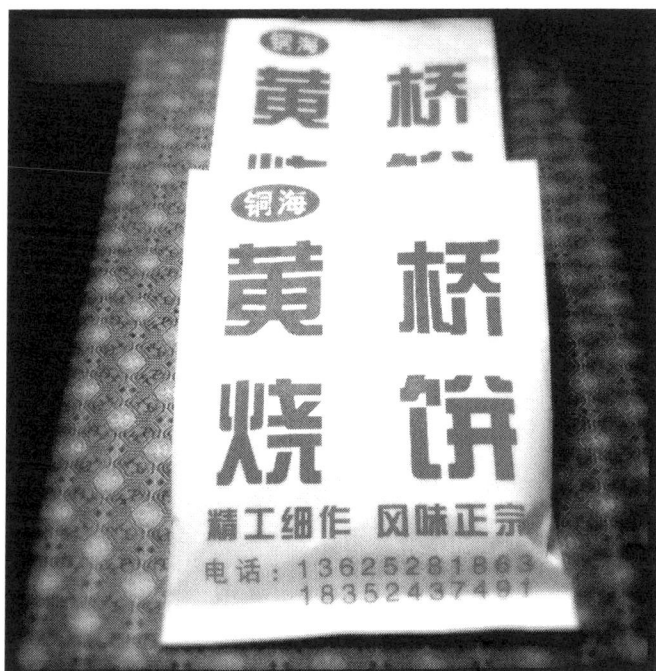

ALL BOOKS ARE IN ENGLISH

スタジオウェナ

有鍐氣

SUTAJIO WENA. BORN IN ASIA. MADE IN USA.

SPRING 2013

春のコレクション

Maxine, Aoki, Beto and Me is a hilarious collection of stories about modern cosmopolitans trying to make the best out of a planet besieged by natural disasters, economic downturns, and political strife. Published in international literary journals in the last two years, these award-winning stories form Wena Poon's third book of globetrotting short fiction. They are published together for the first time with her black and white photography.

Order from Amazon, Baker & Taylor, Ingram, and all major global distributors.
ISBN-10: 1482035308. Available in paperback and Kindle.

SUMMER 2013

夏のコレクション

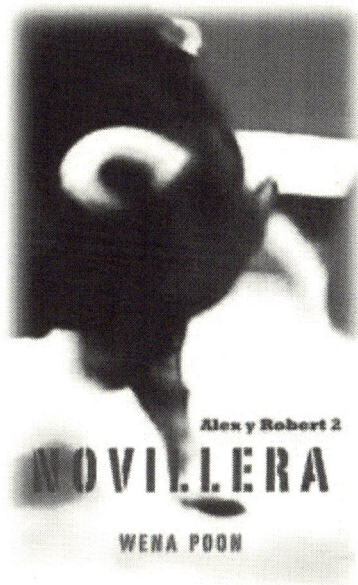

In 2010 the novel *Alex y Robert* was broadcast as a BBC Radio 4 Book at Bedtime. It enchanted British audiences with the unlikely tale of an American woman matador in modern Spain. In order to write *Novillera*, its sequel, Wena Poon left no stone unturned. She trekked across Spain and France, hung out with trainee bullfighters, braved fly-ridden bull ranches, and fought 12 small toros in order to deliver to readers the closest fictional approximation of a front row seat with "crystal-clear surround sound". Featuring original black and white photography shot in and out of the bullring.

Order from Amazon, Baker & Taylor, Ingram, and all major global distributors.
ISBN-10: 1484134699. Available in paperback and Kindle.

FALL 2014

秋のコレクション

The young Emperor Taliesin has been wearing a silver mask ever since he was a child. No one has ever seen his face. Is he really the Son of Heaven? Or a fox spirit in human form? Annoyed by rumors, the Emperor sets off on a quest to prove that he is really human. Only his personal bodyguard, the divine swordswoman Sei Shonagon, knows the truth. *The Adventures of Snow Fox & Sword Girl* is a sophisticated fairy tale in Kurosawa costumes. A wonderfully funny, sexy, swashbuckling romp through the familiar landscape of Chinese and Japanese swordfighting epics, stylishly delivered, as its opening credits promise, "in modern English and in full Technicolor".

WINTER 2014

冬のコレクション

VOYAGE TO THE DARK KIRIN

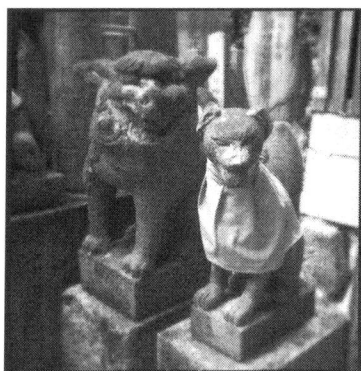

陰影麒麟記

"We are by Nature not a Seafaring People."

Tired of administering his kingdom ever since he was a child, Taliesin, the Son of Heaven and the 33rd Emperor of Jing, decides to max out his budget. He sets sail with a hundred glorious treasure ships to hunt down the mythical black unicorn. "Shonagon's in charge," he announces to the appalled Ministers of Cabinet. Can the divine swordswoman Sei Shonagon outwit Machiavellian dukes, quell unruly ronin, and fight rebellious Noh ninja on her own? Or does she need help from the handsome but terribly prim priest, Takanoha?

Voyage to the Dark Kirin is the second novel of the Hoshimaruhon series, a wonderfully funny, sexy, swashbuckling romp through the familiar landscape of Chinese and Japanese swordfighting epics, stylishly delivered, as its opening credits promise, "in modern English and in full Technicolor". Rated (R) for Adult Themes.

SPRING 2015

春のコレクション

THE MARQUIS OF DISOBEDIENCE

絲
城
違
命
侯

"I have assembled a Cast of Thousands..."

A strange turn of Fate forces Emperor Taliesin to travel incognito in Jing as Scholar Ping: playwright and boy actress, famed for his sexual comedies for the Jing operatic stage. Convinced that she had lost him forever, Sei Shonagon disguises herself as a man and embarks on a mission for a haunted lute that would solve all her problems. Our story takes place nine years after *Voyage to the Dark Kirin* – enough time for the Barbarian Armies to multiply, Lord Paisley to finish building the Great Wall, and Takanoha's adopted daughters to grow up and start rattling their sabers.

The Marquis of Disobedience is the third novel of the Hoshimaruhon series, a wonderfully funny, sexy, swashbuckling romp through the familiar landscape of Chinese literary classics and Japanese samurai epics, stylishly delivered, as its opening credits promise, "in modern English and in full Technicolor". Rated (R) for Adult Themes.

36157602R00087

Made in the USA
Lexington, KY
08 October 2014